Blind Fury

Also by Linda I. Shands
Wild Fire

Wakara of Eagle Lodge

2

Blind Fury

LINDA I. SHANDS

Fleming H. Revell
A Division of Baker Book House Co
Grand Rapids, Michigan 49516

© 2001 by Linda I. Shands

Published by Fleming H. Revell
a division of Baker Book House Company
P.O. Box 6287, Grand Rapids, MI 49516-6287

Printed in the United States of America

All rights reserved. No part of this publication may be reproduced, stored in
a retrieval system, or transmitted in any form or by any means—for example,
electronic, photocopy, recording—without the prior written permission of the
publisher. The only exception is brief quotations in printed reviews.

Library of Congress Cataloging-in-Publication Data

Shands, Linda, 1944-
    Blind fury / Linda I. Shands.
        p.   cm. — (Wakara of Eagle Lodge ; 2)
    Sequel to: Wild fire.
    Summary: After the death of her mother, fifteen-year-old
Wakara and her family, who claim some Yani Indian ancestry, con-
tinue life on their Oregon ranch and face serious challenges when
a sudden blizzard hits.
    ISBN 0-8007-5747-5
    [1. Single-parent families—Fiction. 2. Brothers and sisters—
Fiction. 3. Identity—Fiction. 4. Blizzards—Fiction. 5. Christian life—
Fiction. 6. Ranch life—Oregon—Fiction. 7. Oregon—Fiction.]
I. Title. II. Series: Shands, Linda, 1944- . Wakara of Eagle Lodge ; 2.
PZ7.S52828B1   2001
[Fic]—dc21   00-053361

For current information about all releases from Baker Book House, visit our
web site:

http://www.bakerbooks.com

For

Kaili, Zane,
and Hannah

Acknowledgments

Thank you Elsie Larson and Bobbie Christensen for your time and effort in critiquing this book.

Thank you Mrs. Theodora Kroeber for so beautifully recording Ishi's story.

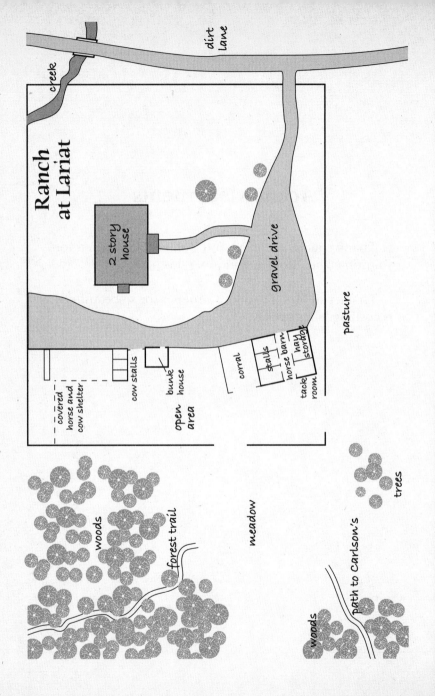

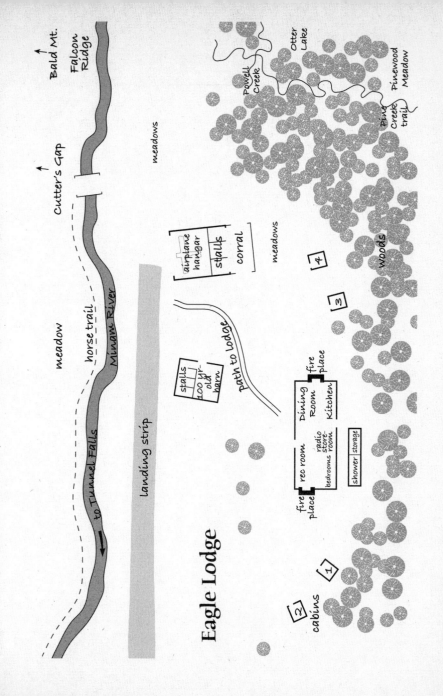

Eagle Lodge

cabins

Bald Mt.
Falcon Ridge

Cutter's Gap

to Tunnel Falls

horse trail

Minam River

meadow

meadow

meadows

meadows

landing strip

airplane hangar

stalls
corral

100 yr. old barn
stalls

path to Lodge

fire place
rec room
radio store-room
bedrooms

Dining Room
Kitchen
fire place

shower | storage

Powell Creek

Otter Lake

Pinewood Meadow

Pine Creek trail

woods

1

"WAKARA WINDSONG SHERIDAN, you haven't heard a word I've said!"

Kara rolled her eyes, tossed another fork full of manure into the wheelbarrow, then turned to her best friend.

"Tia Louise Sanchez, I've heard every word you've said for the past fifteen minutes, but I have to get these stalls cleaned or we won't have any place to put the horses. It's supposed to get down into the thirties tonight."

Tia flashed a guilty smile and set the Internet printouts on the nearest hay bale.

"Sorry. Guess I should be helping, huh? Then maybe we can go up to your room and look at the stuff I found out about your ancestors." She grabbed a shovel and began scooping clean sawdust into Lily's stall.

"My supposed ancestors. Anne could be wrong, you know."

Tia shook her head. "Anne is never wrong. If she says Wakara means *moon* in the Yana language, then she's probably right."

Kara nodded. "I guess so. But that doesn't mean my great-grandmother was from the Yana tribe. The name could have come from anywhere."

She set the rake down long enough to secure her thick, black braid to the top of her head with a banana clip and thought about the drawing hanging on the wall in her bedroom.

Back in 1932, Great-grandfather Harley "Irish" Sheridan had used chalk and charcoal to sketch a picture of his Native American wife. Grandpa Sheridan had given it to Kara along with a few pages from Irish's journal. She looked so much like her ancestor, they'd named her after the first Wakara. Irish's notes said that his fifteen-year-old bride was Nez Perce. That's what the entire family had always believed, until Anne, their Nez Perce cook, had come along and insisted Wakara was a Yana name. Now Wakara's background and Great-grandfather Harley's journal had become a mystery that she and her friend Tia were determined to unravel. In fact, Tia had taken it on as a project for her American History class. When she had discovered how much fun it was to do research on the Internet, she had become obsessed.

Possessed is more like it, Kara thought. She traded the rake for a shovel and began tossing sawdust into the clean stall. As she spread the bedding over the rubber mats, she thought about Anne.

Two years ago, Mom and Dad had bought a guest ranch in the mountains and named it Eagle Lodge. Mom managed the kitchen and four guest cabins, while Dad and Greg took care of the horses and all the repairs needed around the place. Kara helped wherever she was needed. Looking back, she remembered it as being hard work, but fun.

Then Mom died in a car accident, and Dad had hired Anne, a Nez Perce woman from the reservation in Idaho, to run the kitchen at Eagle Lodge. When Anne called Wakara "Little Moon," it was as if she opened the lid on a boiling pot. Kara had been upset at first and wanted to believe Anne was wrong. Then, just three weeks ago, at the end of the summer season, Kara and her little brother had barely escaped from a raging forest fire. After that, she had realized it was who she was on the inside that counted, and she had tried to convince herself it didn't matter if her great-grandmother was Yana or Nez Perce. But in her heart, she knew it did. With Mom gone, Kara felt her heritage mattered very much. In fact, she had finally told her friends and family that Kara was an okay nickname, but she really liked people to call her Wakara.

"Hey, now who's doing all the work?" Tia waved her open palm in front of Kara's eyes.

Kara blinked, then laughed. "Sorry. Guess I was day-dreaming."

"Well you'd better wake up fast." Tia pointed to the door-way of the barn. "Looks like Lily's been rolling."

Lily, Kara's spirited six-year-old quarter horse, thumped at the barn door with a dainty black hoof. Her silky apricot-colored coat was now spattered with thick red-brown mud.

Kara groaned. "I can't believe it—I just groomed her this morning."

Tia reached into the tack box and tossed her a brush. "You groom, I'll finish this stall. Maybe we'll get our home-work done by next Tuesday!"

Kara brushed away the worst of the mud, then led her mare into the clean, dry stall and gave her a pad of hay. As she slid the metal door closed, she heard another horse whinny.

Tia beat her to the door. "It's Colin on Dakota. And Star's right behind them. Looks like we got done just in time."

Colin Jones was Dad's hired hand. He had come here to the ranch in Lariat last spring to help with the string of horses and the small herd of cattle that roamed over their forty acres of land. Colin had spent the summer with them as wrangler at Eagle Lodge, caring for the horses and taking the guests on trail rides. He and her brother Greg were friends, but Colin was also Kara's escort to the football game this weekend. She smiled as she thought about the fun they would have. Who cared if it wasn't a real date? She had another year to go before that. But when she turned fifteen last June, Dad said group dates were okay. The youth group at church was taking a busload of high school kids to the game. Colin wasn't even in high school—he was getting his GED from a junior college, but he was going with them anyway. And she couldn't think of anyone she'd rather hang out with. He was so cute with his hair the color of sun-dried wheat and brown eyes with just the tiniest flecks of green.

"Earth to Wakara. What planet are you on?"

Kara shook away her thoughts and looked up into the real thing—green-flecked eyes sparkling with laughter.

She felt herself turn red from her hair roots to her toenails. "Sorry, Colin. Were you talking to me?"

He tipped his hat. "Well, Ma'am, you're the one blocking the door, and old Dakota here has a hankerin' for his dinner."

Kara grimaced. There was that fake drawl. Between his and her little brother, Ryan's, fascination with old John Wayne movies, she was sick to death of the cowboy routine.

She stepped aside while Colin led Dakota into the stall. Tia hefted a pad of hay into the feeder, while Kara filled the last water bucket and hung it in place.

"Thanks, ladies," Colin drawled as he limped out of the stall. "I sure do appreciate the help."

"No prob." Tia grinned, practically batting her eyelashes at him.

Kara shook her head and smiled. Tia was an outrageous flirt, but everyone knew she didn't mean anything by it. She was just . . . well, just Tia.

Colin coughed and grabbed his ribs. "Ouch. Man, that hurts!"

No kidding! Kara thought. Colin was not supposed to be riding yet—"Give those ribs six weeks at least," the doctor had said, but Colin was as stubborn as an unbridled mule.

Kara and Tia looked at each other. Kara didn't like to think about the forest fire. She and Ryan had escaped with only a few scrapes and bruises, but Colin and Anne had been trapped. They could have been killed. Instead, they had survived, Anne with a broken leg and Colin with a dislocated shoulder, broken ribs, and some smoke damage to his lungs. Kara thanked God every day for saving them.

Star whinnied as a gust of wind whistled through the barn, blowing Ryan in with it.

"Hey, you guys, Dad says to get done and get up to the house. Pronto. There's a big storm coming. He heard it on the radio. Colin, Dad says get the lanterns, 'cause we might lose 'lectricity, and Anne will have to use the camp stove to cook, or we could have cold sandwiches or leftover pizza, and I get to help light the candles with matches from my survival kit." He took a breath and glared at his sister. "I'm old enough. Anne said!"

Kara laughed and threw her hands up in surrender. "Okay, okay. If Anne said it, then it must be all right." Her little brother was growing up, but like Mom had always said, he was an accident waiting to happen. She started to lecture him about using matches only when an adult was around, but he had already grabbed a lantern from the tack room and was running out the door.

Another burst of wind swirled sawdust across the floor. Kara shivered in spite of her heavy sweatshirt and jeans.

15

"I'm out of here," Tia yelled over the noise. "I'm hoofing it, and it's a long way home."

"I don't think you'd better plan on going anywhere," Colin said from the doorway. Kara followed his gaze to the boiling black clouds blowing toward them on heavy gusts of wind. "You girls head for the house. I'll secure the barn and be right there."

Colin was being bossy again, but Kara didn't argue. She helped Tia gather up research papers the wind had scattered, then the two of them sprinted out of the barn and up the gravel drive. They reached the covered porch just as the first heavy drops of rain began to fall.

Anne met them at the door, her leg still encased in a thick, white walking cast. "A short storm, I think," she said, "but a heavy one. We will have some damage this time."

Kara shivered again. Would she ever get used to Anne's predictions? The spookiest thing was, the woman was always right.

Dad had laughed the one time Kara had asked him about it. "There's nothing to be spooked about," he had said. "She just uses common sense. And," he had added, "a lifetime of experience."

Anne's Nez Perce father had been a scholar as well as a farmer. He had seen to it that Anne and her brothers received a good education. He had also written books about Native American history and folklore. Anne had gained a lot of her knowledge from him. Her wisdom, she insisted, came from God.

Tia dashed into the living room, and Kara's dad handed her the phone. Kara could hear the static clear across the room.

"Sure, Pops," Tia yelled into the mouthpiece. "Mr. Sheridan says I can spend the night . . ." A loud POP sounded through the receiver. "Rats, lost him." She handed the phone back to Kara's dad.

16

"Phone lines are down," Colin said as he pushed through the doorway along with Kara's older brother, Greg.

"No doubt," Greg agreed. "Sounded like one of the poles snapped in half." He handed his dripping coat to Anne, but one look from Dad, and he snatched it back. "Sorry," he mumbled. "It's too windy to hang it on the porch."

Anne just nodded. "I'm glad you are home safe." She looked at Colin, who stood holding his own dripping hat and coat. "Put them in the laundry room. The carpet will dry."

Kara breathed a sigh of relief as both of the guys headed toward the kitchen. Two months ago, Greg would have argued and stormed out of the room. But since Dad's friend, Bud Davis, had counseled him, Greg had changed. Kara knew he still missed Mom, but he didn't seem quite as angry anymore.

She felt tears well up and turned toward the window so no one would see. They were all still grieving, including her, but she had to admit things were better than they'd been at first. Once she had gotten over her resentment of Anne and realized the woman wasn't trying to take Mom's place, she was able to let go of some of the burdens she'd been carrying like a sack of rocks around her neck.

Anne had been a big help all summer at Eagle Lodge. After the injuries she'd suffered in the fire had healed enough for her to be released from the hospital, she'd gone for a short visit with her family in Idaho, then come back to help out at the ranch. Ryan loved her, and Kara was grateful to have more time for homework and friends.

The wind blew sheets of rain against the window. Kara gasped as a huge branch snapped off a fir tree, flew through the air, and landed with a thud just inches from the house.

"Wow! That was close." Tia grabbed Kara's arm. "Come on. Your dad wants us to be sure all the upstairs windows are closed."

Another loud CRACK, like an explosion, rocked the house. Kara saw a huge flash of light, and then the room went dark.

"Yeah!" Ryan's excited yelp nearly shattered her eardrums. "Now I get to light the candles."

2

By ten o'clock the rain had turned to sleet. Colin checked on the horses and reported they were doing fine. The barn wasn't new, but it had been built solidly and could stand up to just about anything.

Dad insisted Colin and Greg sleep in the main house instead of the old bunkhouse they were turning into an apartment. "That place could easily fall down around your ears, and I'm sure the plumbing is already frozen," he warned them.

When it had been decided that Anne was to live at the ranch, Dad had given her Greg's room. Greg was just as happy rooming with Colin in the bunkhouse, even though Anne couldn't climb the stairs to Greg's room right now because of her cast. She'd been sleeping in the recliner in the living room.

"We should all sleep downstairs tonight," Dad said. "Ryan can have the couch. The boys and I will use sleeping bags on the floor and take turns keeping the fire going." He looked at Wakara. "It's up to you, Sugar Bear, but I think you and Tia will be better off down here with us. It's freezing upstairs."

Tia's eyes brightened. "Cool. Lots of Indian tribes slept in community lodges to keep from freezing in the winter." She looked to Anne for confirmation, and Anne nodded.

"You have studied well," Anne said.

Kara couldn't help matching her friend's proud grin. Tia had studied hard after getting an F in American History and had brought her grade up to a B.

Kara's stomach did a nosedive as she listened to ice crystals pelt the side of the house. The game! It was tomorrow night. What if school was canceled, or the roads were washed out, and they couldn't go?

She felt Anne's arm slip around her shoulders and give a gentle squeeze. "This storm will pass by morning."

Once again the woman had managed to read her thoughts, but Kara was grateful for the encouragement, and for the comfort of a hug.

If only Anne were Mom. She pushed the thought away and prayed Anne couldn't see it in her face. Yet somehow she didn't think Anne would be offended.

Kara fell asleep right away, but when the lights snapped on at 5 A.M., she groaned and scrunched farther down in her sleeping bag, burying her head and eyes. In spite of their best intentions, the fire had gone out during the night and the room felt like a walk-in freezer. When warm air began to blow through the heat registers, someone got up and flicked off the lights.

Two hours later, Kara felt a light touch on her shoulder as Anne's voice roused her from her dreams. "Get up, please. School begins at ten o'clock."

She yawned and crawled out of her sleeping bag, grateful for the warmth that greeted her. "Thanks, Anne. I'll take a shower and help you with breakfast."

Anne smiled. "No need. The others have eaten. Only two birds stay late in their nests."

Tia sat up and blinked. "Where'd everybody go?"

"The men check the stock. Ryan is upstairs. He could use some help, I think." She moved back toward the kitchen as the unmistakable sounds of gunfire and hoofbeats echoed down the stairs.

Tia giggled. "You mean, he needs a kick in the—"

"She means," Kara interrupted, "he needs some redirection. He knows he's not supposed to watch John Wayne on a school morning."

"Thank you Psych 101." Tia scrambled out of her bedroll and headed for the stairs. "You redirect, and I'll hit the shower."

By the time Kara dressed, ate breakfast, and fed Lily, sunlight danced across the soggy fields. Most of the ice from last night's storm had melted. Out here everyone took the same school bus, and Ryan ran ahead of Kara and Tia as far as the footbridge. "Wow! Look! It's really flooding." He pushed up onto the railing and balanced on his belly to see under the bridge.

Kara's heart did a flip. The image of her little brother falling partway over the cliff at Tunnel Falls was still fresh in her memory. Evidently he hadn't learned any lessons. She fought the urge to yell, but jogged to the bridge and grabbed the back of his pants. She yanked hard and pulled him off the railing, scraping his belly on the rough wood.

"Ow! Stop that!" he yelled.

She wanted to shake him. Instead she took a deep breath, counted to ten, and let it out. "Ryan Sheridan, when are you going to learn . . . ?" The look on his face stopped her.

"I-I-I'm s-sorry, Kara. I won't do it again, I promise." He flung his arms around her legs, and she could feel his body shaking.

Tia ran up, breathing like a steam engine. She flashed Kara a mixed look of panic and relief, and pointed toward

21

the crossroad. "The bus is coming, you guys. We'd better hustle if we want a ride." She tugged on Ryan's arm and led him across the bridge.

"What am I going to do with him, Mom?" Kara whispered. "One of these days he's going to get into real trouble, and I won't be able to help him."

Let go and get a grip on God. A picture of the bumper sticker on Colin's pickup flashed into her mind.

She swiped at a tear that was dripping off her nose and hurried to the waiting bus.

The only class she missed that day was American Government, which to Wakara was no big loss. English was her favorite. They were writing short stories this term, and she had formed a plot based on her summer experience with the forest fire.

Mr. Jaminson had even asked her to share some of her survival techniques in Health and Safety. That was harder. She talked about how she had soaked a bandanna in the river and tied it around her nose and mouth to filter the smoke, then explained how they had rationed drinking water and used smoke signals to attract attention from the planes. When she was done, Mr. Jaminson led the class in applause and said, "Well, young lady, how does it feel to be a hero?"

Kara took a deep breath. Could she really tell the truth? The kids might laugh, but she knew she had to try.

"It wasn't me, Mr. Jaminson." She turned back to face the class. "God is the real hero. He's the one who showed me where to go and what to do. If I hadn't prayed and asked Him to show me the way out, we would never have found the path under the ledge. And without God, I would never have had the courage to look for it."

Some of the kids snickered. A few nodded. Most just looked down at their desks. Mr. Jaminson cleared his throat.

"Uh, thank you, Wakara." But as she passed him to get to her seat, he smiled and whispered, "You have more courage than you think."

Right, she thought. *Then why are my hands shaking?*

By the time the last bell rang, all Kara could think about was the football game—and if she was really honest, her group date with Colin. The church bus was leaving at four o'clock. They still had to change and grab a bite to eat. She joined Tia in a cheer when they saw the car. "All right! Mom to the rescue!"

Ryan was already buckled into the front seat, so she squeezed into the back with Tia. "Thanks, Mrs. Sanchez, this will really save us some time."

"No problem." Tia's mom put the car in gear and turned left onto Center Street. "Your bags are in the trunk. You can change at the church. Wakara, your dad sent along wool socks and a warm jacket. It's going to get cold again tonight."

Tia sniffed. "Hey, food!"

"Superburgers!" Ryan hefted a white bag over his head. "I get one too."

His tone dared anyone to say otherwise, and Kara laughed along with the rest. She couldn't say he'd ruin his dinner, because she knew it wasn't true. Her little brother ate like a linebacker and stayed skinny as a twig.

Colin met them at the church. He seemed really glad to see her, but was kind of quiet on the two-hour bus ride to the game. *Who can blame him?* Kara thought. *It's not like he knows anybody but Tia and me.* And Tia was no help. She sat across from them chattering a hundred miles an hour with her boyfriend, Devon. Most of the others were just as hyper. Kara heard more than she wanted to know about Brian— "Slip and Slide"—Coleman. The new quarterback was supposed to be a superstar. According to most of the kids, he was meaner than a rattlesnake and faster than a cobra.

"I'll believe it when I see it," Colin muttered. "If he's that slippery he probably won't be able to hang on to the ball." He flashed Kara a grin, scooted down in the seat, and pulled his hat over his eyes.

Kara steamed silently. *Fine, if Colin Jones wants to be rude, I can just ignore him.*

Colin was quiet for most of the game. He kept getting up to buy food, or just walk around behind the bleachers. "You don't need to come," he told her at least five times. "I'll be back in a minute."

By the last quarter, everyone was huddled together on the bleachers, shivering from the icy wind that blew through the outdoor field. Wakara wished the game would end so they could take off. "Slip and Slide" Coleman had just fumbled for the second time, and the scoreboard showed 14 to 0 against Lariat with five minutes to go in the game.

Colin snorted, washed down his hot dog with the last of his Coke and gathered up the trash. "I'll bag this stuff and meet you at the bus," he told Kara.

Kara bit her lip and held back the tears. He'd been a first-class jerk all evening. What had happened to the cool guy who had asked to be her escort for the game? "It's not like I forced him to come," she muttered to herself.

Tia nudged her. "Colin's got the right idea. Let's go back to the bus. At least it'll be warmer in there."

Kara practically jumped up the three steps into the bus. Colin was in the back talking to Mr. Andrews. Scratch that. Mr. Andrews was doing the talking. Colin was listening and nodding with the strangest look on his face.

She'd seen that look before, but on Dad's face, not Colin's. Dad had been standing on the deck at Eagle Lodge, staring out over the meadow past the river, his mouth twisted in a weird half-smile, like he was listening for something. "Pensive" Anne had called it. She knew without a doubt Dad

24

had been dreaming about her mother. Who, or what, was Colin thinking about?

Kara's anger melted as fast as an April snow. Colin had definitely been acting weird tonight, but he wasn't being deliberately mean. Something was bothering him. He'd lost both his parents to alcohol and divorce; maybe he was thinking about them. She could tell his ribs and shoulder were hurting from the cold. Sitting on those hard bleachers must have been torture. She should have realized he'd be uncomfortable, not to mention bored out of his mind.

"Penny for your thoughts." Colin pulled off his gloves and laid a hand against her cheek. "Whoa. You're really cold."

Act like nothing's wrong, Wako, or you'll just make it worse. "I'm fine." Her voice sounded like fingernails on a blackboard. She swallowed hard and tried again. "I'll warm up. Want the window seat?"

Colin shook his head. "Nah. The aisle's fine." He eased into the seat next to her with a soft moan. "I'm sorry, Wakara. I know I haven't been much company tonight. Guess I haven't healed as well as I thought."

His face was pale and his eyes, when she looked into them, were bright with pain.

3

On Saturday morning, Dad took one look at Colin and ordered him to bed in Ryan's room. "You're down for the weekend, young man. Greg and I leave Monday morning for Eagle Lodge. I need you well enough to ride. If we're going to get those cows down out of the high country before winter hits, it's got to be soon, and I'm counting on you to get it done."

He sounded stern, but Kara saw the worry on his face.

Colin didn't argue, and she felt even guiltier about last night.

"He wouldn't have gone if it wasn't for me," she e-mailed Tia. "The least I can do is handle the barn chores. Sorry, I know you wanted to show me your research stuff. Maybe tomorrow afternoon after church, okay?"

Kara groomed Dakota first. Lily was content to wait, but Ryan's pony, Star, nickered for attention. He was eighteen years old and gentle as a lamb, but she knew Ryan would soon outgrow him. Eighteen was too old to be kept outside with the working string, but they would probably still take him up to the lodge in the summer for the little kids to ride.

She finished picking Dakota's huge feet, then put a halter on Star. "Your turn." She scratched behind his ears, then picked up a clean, soft brush. "Ryan should be doing this, you know." The pony tossed his head. He knew Ryan's name, all right. When Dad had bought him two years ago for Ryan's birthday, it had been love at first sight for both of them.

But her little brother had gone to his friend Timmy's today. Timmy's family had been a godsend since Mom had died, keeping Ryan busy, even taking him on outings with their family. Lately, Ryan spent part of every weekend at their house.

She patted Star's rump, and he trotted out of the barn to join Dakota in the paddock. Ryan would be seven years old in November. Dad had always told them, "If you're old enough to ride, you're old enough to take care of your horse." But with all the work of opening Eagle Lodge this summer, the grief over Mom's death, and then the forest fire, they had let Ryan's responsibilities slide. *Next Saturday,* she decided, *Ryan will start learning to take care of his own horse.*

She had just started to brush out Lily's mane, when the mare shied and danced off the mat. Kara took hold of the bridle to quiet her as an ancient Ford pickup rattled into the yard. The truck bed was full of plywood and bundles of insulation.

"Sorry, Wakara," Bud Davis called over the din of the idling engine, "didn't mean to spook your horse, but your dad said he needed this stuff pronto. Know where he's at?"

Kara steadied Lily with one hand and pointed up the hill. "In the bunkhouse. He and Greg are trying to get it into shape for winter."

"Where's Colin?"

She felt her face go red. "In bed. He's still in too much pain to work."

27

Bud frowned. "Well, maybe I'll just go on up there and see what I can do to help."

He would, too. Bud Davis was a longtime family friend. He had helped with more than one mess—including Greg. Greg's life was headed for the garbage can until Bud counseled him. After that, Kara's older brother had finally dealt with his grief and let God work in his life. Things weren't perfect. Greg was eighteen and could still be a pain, but he'd quit drinking and had stayed away from T. J. Magic and his gang.

The pickup rattled its way up the gravel drive. She had just settled Lily back into position on the grooming mat when she heard hoofbeats. Lily danced and whinnied, eager to greet Tia's horse, Patches, as Tia rode him into the yard.

"Hey." Tia waved and dismounted, tying Patches to a post outside the barn. "Want some help? Pops is watching football, and Mom went grocery shopping." She wrinkled her nose. "I'd rather help you clean the stalls so we can ride."

Kara laughed and nodded toward the tack room. "You know where the rakes are."

Leave it to Tia. Only she could find a way to make shoveling manure fun. Tia could drive you crazy, but Kara knew she'd never find a better friend.

With Dad and Greg working and Colin stuck in bed, Kara felt a little guilty as she saddled Lily for a ride. But the guilt feelings didn't last for long. When she was riding Lily, everything else just faded into the background. Her horse was spirited and strong, but gentle, and responded instantly to her every cue.

The wind had a nip to it as they jogged through the field behind the barn. Kara stopped long enough to zip her jacket, then she and Tia urged their horses into a run. Lily won the race as usual, but this time Patches was practically on her heels.

"Whew, almost got you that time," Tia chortled as they slowed to a walk.

Kara reached over and patted the pretty paint. "You must be feeding him that special grain mixture again. He's not even blowing hard!"

Tia grinned. "Pops thinks Patches and I are ready to start barrel racing."

She looked at Wakara with that pleading look, and Kara groaned. She knew what was coming; she could almost repeat it by heart.

"Please? You know I don't want to do it alone. Come on, Wakara, at least try it. Or team penning!" Her eyes lit up with this new idea. "Lily and Patches are so used to each other, and they both love cows—we'd be a cinch to take ribbons in that event."

Kara couldn't help but feel a surge of excitement. It would be fun. And Tia was right. Lily and Patches would clean house. Then she came back to reality.

"You know I can't," she said softly. "I have to help Dad at Eagle Lodge all next summer. That knocks out most of the local competitions. And I sure don't have time to travel for the rodeo circuit."

She hated the doomed look on Tia's face. "Sorry. You know I'll help you practice. Patches will be a great barrel racer, and you'll be bringing home all the ribbons on your own."

Tia shrugged and dropped behind as they entered the narrow trail that wound into the woods. Kara inhaled the fresh smell of pine. They ducked under tree limbs and stepped over branches felled by the storm. She hated to disappoint her best friend, but Tia had to understand that family came first. Her dad had made it clear he couldn't run Eagle Lodge without her. Or the ranch either for that matter. Sure, they had Anne now. And that was a big help. But with Mom gone, there was so much to do . . .

Kara's thoughts turned to the trail. "If we want to ride this winter, we'd better get out here and get some of these branches picked up," she called back to Tia.

When there was no answer, Kara looked over her shoulder. Tia was stopped about twenty yards back, looking into the woods and trying to keep Patches from throwing his head.

"What is it? What's wrong?" Kara called.

Tia spun Patches around and urged him up the trail toward them. Lily's ears went up, and she began to sidestep nervously. Kara rubbed Lily's neck to calm her.

Tia's face was pale as a ghost. "Tia, you're scaring me. What did you see?"

"I don't know," Tia panted. "Patches stopped and didn't want to budge. Then I saw the branches move, but I couldn't see anything." She tightened up on the reins. "He's still spooked. Something's out there."

Stay calm. "Stay calm." She said it aloud. "If we get upset, the horses will too."

Lily's ears went back as she flung her head. Kara felt the mare's muscles tense and knew she was getting ready to rear. She put all her concentration into keeping Lily's head down.

Lily spun in circles, not wanting to go forward or back. Patches was just as bad, practically climbing onto Lily's back. They were spooking each other, and Kara wasn't sure what to do.

There is nothing to fear but fear itself. Where had she heard that? *Lord, I'm really afraid. Please calm me down and show me what to do.*

Lily spun forward and raced up the trail, taking twists and turns without a pause and jumping over fallen limbs. Kara hung on with all her might and prayed that Tia and Patches were right behind her—she couldn't hear a thing over the sound of her own heartbeat rushing in her ears.

Her stomach jumped in fear when she realized Devil's Creek was dead ahead. The creek was usually just bridle deep and about six feet wide, but now it was more like a river, swollen with floodwater from the recent storm. If Lily plunged them into the current, there was no doubt in Kara's mind they would drown.

Tia screamed, "Look out!"

Like I have any control! But Kara sat up a little and eased back on the reins. Lily came to a stop only inches from the raging water.

Patches skidded to a stop beside them. Tia didn't waste any time, and jumped to the ground. Kara felt Lily settle under her, blowing and snorting from exertion. She took her feet out of the stirrups and slid to the ground beside Tia, holding tight to her horse's bridle. Patches blew and pawed the earth.

Kara realized her legs were shaking. She led Lily to a tree and tied her, yanking on the knot to be sure it was secure, then she plopped down on a large, flat rock. Tia sat next to her, tears running in rivulets down her cheeks.

Kara slipped an arm around her friend's shoulders. When she could breathe again, she followed Tia's anxious gaze back down the trail. "What was that all about?"

Tia shuddered. "I don't know. Something was in there." Her face tightened in fear. "What if it was a bear? Pops said the Carlsons had one rooting through their garbage the other night."

Kara nodded and frowned. "I guess. For all we know it could have been a raccoon."

Tia straightened her shoulders. "Patches wouldn't spook over a raccoon. Besides, you know as well as I do that raccoons are nocturnal. They only come out at night."

Kara pulled her arm away. "A horse will spook over anything under the right conditions, Tia Sanchez, and for all we know it could have been a rabid raccoon. Then it wouldn't care if it was day or night. Anyway, it was Patches who started the whole thing. Lily didn't panic until he did."

"Oh, great, now it's all my fault!"

Kara's stomach did a flip, and she felt like she would lose her breakfast any minute. "Tia, I'm sorry. That's not what I meant."

Tia sniffed, then started laughing. "Listen to us. A rabid raccoon? We sound like a couple of five-year-olds."

Kara laughed with her until she had to wipe away her own tears. "Whew. That was close."

"Now what?" Tia's voice still trembled.

Kara looked around. They were in a large clearing surrounded by trees on two sides, with the creek in front of them and the trail behind. "No way we're crossing that creek today. And I don't know about you, but I'm not excited about going the long way around." Going off-trail would take them deep into the woods before they hit ranch property. Kara had walked that way often when she and Mom went foraging for berries. But navigating it on horseback was another matter. Not to mention the fact that whatever had spooked the horses might still be around.

"I say we sit tight and wait for your dad to send the cavalry," Tia said.

"Oh, sure. That could be next week. When he and Greg are working on a project, they haven't got a clue about time."

"Well, I'm not going back there!" Tia pointed down the trail. "If Patches bolts again, I'm too tired to hang on."

Tia was right. So what were they going to do?

A clear head unmuddies many waters.

Another one of Anne's sayings. Kara walked a few feet down the trail and stood still.

Listen to the birds. They tell when danger is near.

That one had puzzled her at first until she understood what Anne meant. When the birds are quiet or suddenly fly away, beware!

It was silent now. The skin on Kara's arms prickled. She scanned the treetops. Not a bird in sight.

The wind that had ruffled her hair as they rode now rustled through the pine boughs, moaning like a ghost.

Stop it! She scolded herself. Now was definitely not the time to let her imagination play tricks on her.

She turned around and forced herself to walk calmly back to where Tia waited in the clearing. The horses were pulling at their tethers, looking longingly at the water rolling over the banks of the creek.

Kara began untying Lily's reins. "Come on. They've rested long enough. We can water them now."

Tia rubbed her hand down Patches' sweat-slick neck. "He's still a little warm, but his breathing is fine. I guess they do need a drink."

They led the horses to the creek and let them drink their fill. Then Kara dug into her saddlebag and pulled out two packs of juice. "Here." She handed one to Tia. "We need a drink too. It's going to be a long walk back."

"Walk!" Tia nearly swallowed her straw.

"Sure. We lead the horses and stay alert. I'll go first, and you keep an eye on Lily's ears. If she starts twitching them like radar, we let go and follow them out of there."

She found two sturdy sticks and handed one to Tia. "We can use these if we need a weapon. Smack the bushes and make lots of noise. Patches and Lily won't shy as long as we stay in control."

Tia looked reluctant, but Kara didn't plan on giving her time to think about it. She turned Lily's head and began leading her down the trail, beating her stick against the trees

33

and singing at the top of her lungs, "George, George, king of the jungle. Watch out for that tree." She heard Tia laugh, then join in, half yelling, half singing the silly song.

A hundred yards down the trail Kara's throat was already sore from shouting. She'd about decided to change the tone and the song when Lily came to an abrupt halt.

"Wakara?" Tia's voice squeaked like a mouse caught in a trap.

"Shh. Listen." Kara studied the woods and the trail in front of them, but heard and saw nothing.

Suddenly, Lily bolted. Kara dropped the reins and jumped out of the way as her horse galloped off down the trail, Patches right behind her. Tia had stumbled into the bushes and was just picking herself up when the zing of a rifle shot sent her back to the ground. Kara dove after her, her heart pounding so hard she couldn't breathe. Tia's screams scared her more than the single shot or the loss of their horses.

"Tia! Are you hit?" Wakara tried to turn her over. Tia's eyes were squeezed shut and she wouldn't budge, but she kept screaming. Kara fought to keep her voice steady. "Tia, you're scaring me. Please calm down and let me see."

Tia's screams subsided to frantic sobs, and Kara succeeded in getting her to roll over on her back. "Where does it hurt? Show me." She ran her hands down her friend's arms and legs, then unzipped Tia's jacket. No blood.

The crack of branches and boots pounding on the trail sent Kara's pulse into overdrive. Male voices echoed through the trees. "This way. The screams came from behind those trees."

Kara froze, her mind racing along with her heart. Were escaped criminals attacking them? Maybe poachers? No, not poachers, hunting season started yesterday. But this was private land. She crawled closer to the trail to get a better look.

The men were only a few yards away and walking fast. It took her two seconds to recognize Dennis Carlson and his brother, Davie, sixteen-year-old twins whose father owned a neighboring ranch.

"Wakara?" Dennis ran over and leaned his rifle against a tree. Then he spotted Tia. His eyes widened with fear. "Is she okay? I mean, we didn't hit her, did we?" He shook his head. "We couldn't have."

Davie ran up behind his brother, panting almost as hard as the black lab that followed at his heels. The dog headed straight for Tia and gave her face a thorough washing. Davie finally got hold of his collar and pulled him off. "No, Duke, that's enough, boy."

The dog came willingly, and Tia sat up. "Yuck. Oh, gross. David Carlson, you keep that dog away from me!"

"See, she's not shot." Dennis howled in relief. "Holy Malony! Scared the spit out of me."

Davie whacked his brother on the arm. "Watch your mouth, there's ladies present."

Dennis ignored him and turned to Wakara. "I only fired one shot, but it missed. I know, because Davie and me saw that old cougar take off, and it weren't anywhere near in this direction."

4

WAKARA TOOK A DEEP BREATH of crisp fall air and settled on the top porch step, letting her gaze scan the rich, green pastureland. Beyond her field of vision, the desert spread out dust brown and barren. But here the land had been cultivated for ranches that backed up against majestic mountains, some of which were snowcapped all year long. The forty acres of pasture where they grazed horses and wintered the cattle were dotted with wild apple trees. Right now the trees were surrounded by makeshift fences to keep the horses from gorging on the fruit. Lily and Dakota would eat apples until they made themselves sick.

Kara's stomach rumbled. She'd been too exhausted to eat much supper last night, and the sick feeling she'd had since their adventure yesterday had lasted all through breakfast and church this morning.

It had been a close call. Dad hadn't been pleased with her decision to walk and lead the horses. "You would have been safer in the saddle, even if they bolted," he had reasoned. "It's doubtful a cougar would chase down a galloping horse and rider, even if it were really hungry. But it might have gone after one of you girls."

The screen door slammed, and Ryan came up behind her. "When's Dad coming home?"

"Probably not until tomorrow."

"No fair! Dad promised we could have ice cream after church."

"They had to go up the mountain and round up the herd; you know that, Ry." Dad didn't want to take chances on that cat getting to the cattle, so he and Greg had taken off at dawn.

Ryan ran to the driveway and started kicking rocks. When he picked up a large rock and threw it into the pasture, she knew she had to intervene.

"Ryan Sheridan, stop that! What if you'd hit Star?"

Ryan stomped toward the porch. "I wasn't going to hit ole Star! Anyway, I never get to ride him 'cause I can't ride alone, and no one ever wants to go with me."

Kara flinched. He had a point. Anne couldn't ride with her leg still in a cast, and the men had their days filled with chores. That left her to take care of Ryan, and she'd been so busy with school and her own chores, she had forgotten that he needed a companion to ride Star. It was a good rule, especially for an accident magnet like her brother, but it was a real pain.

Ryan stormed into the house, ran up to his bedroom, and shut the door. She was about to follow him when the phone rang.

"Wakara!" Tia sounded breathless. "You won't believe this. I found them! Your ancestors. Right here on page eight. This is so cool! And, get this—Wakara isn't a real name, it's a nickname, and Anne was only partly right; it means *Full Moon*, not *Little Moon*."

"Tia, slow down. You sound like Ryan."

"Sorry, but you've got to see this. Pops said I can come over, if it's okay with your dad."

Kara hesitated only a second. She really needed to have a talk with Ry, but what if Tia had really found a record of the first Wakara? That would be so awesome!

"Dad's not here," she said. "Neither is Greg. Can your dad bring you over?"

"Mom already said she would. See you in a few."

Kara hung up and went into the kitchen. She washed her hands, then helped herself to a bowl of homemade vegetable soup. Anne's cooking was hard to resist. *Like Mom's.* No one could ever take Mom's place, and Kara knew Anne would never try, but the Nez Perce woman sure ran a close second.

Ten minutes later, Anne set a dish of pie á la mode in front of Kara and another beside her. As if on cue, Tia dashed through the door.

"Cool, I missed dessert at home. Thanks, Anne." She grinned and joined Kara at the table.

Kara stared at Anne, but she was already at the sink rinsing dishes. *How did she know? I never told her Tia was coming.*

Tia interrupted her thoughts. "Eat fast, I want you to see this. You too, Anne. It's all right here in this book. I'm so excited I could have a coronary or something."

"Ah. You found Mrs. Kroeber's book," Anne said without turning around.

Tia swallowed a mouthful of pie. "Yeah. Theodora Kroeber. How'd you know?" She handed the book to Wakara.

"*ISHI—Last of His Tribe.*" Kara read the title out loud.

Anne dried her hands and joined them at the table. "Mrs. Kroeber tells well the story of Ishi and his family. But he was not really the last of the Yahi-Yana tribe."

Tia nodded. "That's what the stuff I got off the Internet says."

"All right, you guys. Let me in on this, okay?" Kara frowned. "I think I've read something about this Ishi. Isn't he the guy they found starving to death in California, way back in the early 1900s?"

"Right!" Tia pushed her pie plate away and grabbed some papers out of her book bag. "They didn't know what to do with him, so they fed him and put him in jail. Then some professor or something came and said he was a Yahi Indian, so they took him to San Francisco and put him in a museum.

"Not on display, though. He lived and worked there. He helped them understand some of the Yahi language and culture."

Kara looked at Anne. "He's pretty famous, isn't he? Your father recorded his story in his book." She frowned. "But I still don't understand what that has to do with me."

"She moves in quietness as does the moon," Anne said softly.

Kara shivered. "What does that mean?"

Tia grabbed the book, opened it, and shoved it back in front of her. "It's your name. Wakara. Right there on page eight."

Kara couldn't believe her eyes. "It says this Ishi's father called his wife Wakara, Full Moon, because 'she moves in quietness as does the moon.' Does that mean this Ishi's mother is my great-grandmother?" She thought a minute, then shook her head. "That doesn't make any sense. According to Irish's journal, he found his Wakara as a newborn baby. Her mother had been shot, and died before she could tell him anything but the baby's name."

She picked up the book and flipped through the pages. "Besides, the timing isn't right."

39

"So?" Tia gave her a disgusted look. "Ishi's mother could have passed the name down, don't you see?" She pointed to the book. "What about his cousin, Tushi? Maybe she didn't die. Maybe she really ran away and joined another tribe. She could have had a baby and named her Wakara after the woman who raised her. It could have happened that way, couldn't it, Anne?"

Anne shook her head. "The lost ones were never found."

Kara looked from Anne to Tia. "Wait a minute. Who are the lost ones?"

"Ishi's uncle and cousin. They ran off to hide when some white men found their cave. When they didn't come back, Ishi went to look for them. He found Tushi's necklace near the place where they would cross the river to get to the hidden shelter, but he never found her or his uncle."

Tia's head drooped and she turned back to Anne. "So you think they fell off the log and drowned?"

"This is what Ishi believed."

"Then how did Wakara's great-grandmother get the name? Ishi's mother was too old to be her. Anyway, it says here she died the next winter." She flipped to the back of the book. "That would have been about 1908. Irish Sheridan wrote that he found the baby, Wakara, and her mother nine years later, in 1917."

"From what I read," Kara broke in, "most of the tribes in that part of California were wiped out during the gold rush days."

Anne nodded. "That is true. But not all died."

"That's right!" Tia grabbed her backpack and started digging through the mess of books and papers. "Some of the Indians were captured and sold as slaves, and some of them went to live on reservations, mixed in with other tribes.

40

"Where's my other book?" She turned the backpack upside down and shook everything out onto the table. "It's in here somewhere. Don't you see? We just have to check the dates and do a little more research. Man!" Tia collapsed back into her chair, eyes sparkling like she'd found her own gold mine. "We are so close. Like, we are HOT! You could have relatives still out there."

Kara's head suddenly throbbed. She rested it in her hands and closed her eyes. "Now I'm really confused. I thought Irish Sheridan found Wakara somewhere here in Oregon. Didn't these Yahi people live in Northern California?"

She felt Anne's hands on her shoulders. The sturdy fingers began massaging her neck. "It is enough, for now, to know the origin of your name. The rest of the mystery will wait."

Tia took the hint and pushed back from the table. "Sorry, I thought it would make you happy."

"I'm sorry too." Tia was right, she should be ecstatic to find out where her name really came from. Instead, she felt frustrated and sad. This latest information only added new pieces to the puzzle.

Tia stuffed papers and junk back into her bag. Kara picked up the book about Ishi. "Look, I do appreciate all the research you've done. Can I keep the book and read it this week?"

"Sure. I got it from the school library, if you can believe that. It's been under our noses all along."

Tia's mom came for her at eight o'clock. In spite of Anne's massage, Kara felt like her head was going to burst.

Anne had already gone into the family room, where she spent most evenings. Dad had insisted she use that space for privacy until she could climb the stairs.

41

Kara turned the locks on the doors, checked the thermostat, and headed up the stairs. At the landing, she could see light coming from under Ryan's door.

"Ry?" She tapped on the door, then opened it and peeked in. Ryan was sprawled on his stomach facing the foot of his bed, munching butterscotch candy and flipping the pages of a book.

"Shh." He put his finger to his lips and pointed to the other twin bed. "Colin's sleeping," he whispered.

No wonder Ryan had been so quiet all evening. He'd had Colin for company, even if Colin was flat on his back, still dressed in dirty jeans and a sweat-stained shirt, with his hat pulled over his eyes. He was snoring like an asthmatic frog.

She stifled a giggle and motioned Ryan out of the room. "Is it okay if he spends the night? I don't think Dad and Greg got the bunkhouse finished."

Ryan nodded soberly. "Sure," he said in a normal voice. "He was helping me with my letters, but then he fell asleep. Right in the middle of capital Ns."

"Shh!" She put one finger to her lips and glanced at the bed. Colin's breathing changed, but he didn't move. She groaned, then clapped a hand over her mouth. She felt like roadkill, but if Ryan hadn't finished his homework, she would have to help him.

"It's okay, Miss Kara, you can go to bed now; we men have got it handled."

Colin hadn't moved, but his hat had shifted to a different angle, and she could see one corner of his lip twitch.

It took her five seconds to snag a pillow and smack him in the head.

It took Colin three seconds to grab her arms and pin her to the mattress.

"Ha, Kara. Colin won." Ryan danced around the room throwing make-believe punches.

Kara didn't even bother to struggle. By the time Colin let her up she was seeing stars. He was groaning and holding his ribs. "Truce," he gasped.

"Truce," she agreed. Her headache was so bad she felt like she was going to pass out. The next thing she knew, she was in her own bed. Colin was leaning over her, wiping her face with cool cloths, while Anne called instructions from the floor below.

5

WHEN THE ALARM WENT OFF at 6:30, Wakara's headache was gone, but it threatened to grab her again when she remembered Colin bending over her, his eyes filled with concern. He must have picked her up off the floor and carried her into her room.

She groaned. How totally embarrassing! She had never fainted in her life, and she had to go and pass out practically in Colin's arms.

To her relief, the only one at breakfast was Ryan.

By the time she had swallowed a few bites of toast and managed to convince Anne she felt well enough to go to school, she and Ryan had to run to catch the bus. She had tests in both of her morning classes and didn't get a break until after Health and Safety, when Mr. Jaminson pulled her aside.

"You won't believe this," she told Tia at lunchtime. "Mr. Jaminson, my Health teacher, wants Colin and me to do a survival demonstration for a class field trip!"

Tia's brown eyes practically popped out of their sockets. "Cool! What did Colin say?"

"I haven't asked him yet, but I think he'll say yes." She remembered the way he had bent over her last night, his eyes full of worry, but his lips twitching in a teasing smile. She couldn't stop the blush that crept from her forehead to her chin, and hurried on before Tia could pick up on it. "They have a curriculum. It's really for pilots who survive airplane crashes, but it will be easy to adapt. We just have to work out a presentation. It can't be too hard. These kids are all our age."

Tia laughed. "Right. And most of them can't survive a day without pizza."

Kara thought about it all the way home. Maybe she should have had Mr. Jaminson ask for Colin's help instead of volunteering to ask him herself. The class wasn't something she wanted to tackle on her own, and with Colin's experience in Alaska, he was the most logical choice for an assistant. But what if he said no?

Her breath blew steam into the cold air as she crossed the footbridge onto their dirt road. Even before she reached the gravel drive, she heard the low of cattle from the front pasture.

"Dad's home!" Ryan sprinted toward the house.

She let him go. He needed to run and get rid of some of that energy.

A few minutes later, she set her books on the table by the stairway. The smell of coffee and Ryan's excited chatter drew her into the kitchen. Dad, Colin, and Greg were gathered around the kitchen table munching cookies. Ryan had draped himself over Dad's shoulder, asking questions and pointing to the map laid out on the center of the table.

"Hi, Sugar Bear." Dad's smile was genuine, but she could tell he was tired by the way his eyelids drooped.

She reached around Ryan to give Dad a hug and a kiss on the cheek. "I'm glad you're home." She had a million questions herself, starting with why they were studying a topography map of the Blue Mountains.

She took the seat next to Dad. Anne handed her a cup of coffee, and Colin pushed the plate of snickerdoodles in her direction. An uneasy feeling stirred in her chest. Dad and Greg were supposed to make repairs at Eagle Lodge this week, but the cattle drive had delayed the trip. With that, and the unpredictable weather, she had assumed they had changed their plans. But the map could only mean one thing.

Dad spoke up before she could ask. "Greg and I were just going over the terrain around Cutter's Gap Wilderness. Hunting's been banned in there this year because of the fire, but we're already booked solid for next season—the new growth will be perfect for elk."

Kara loved coffee, but the sip she took tasted bitter. Dad kept his eyes on the map. He knew how she felt about the hunting trips. It meant that Dad and Greg were gone four to six weeks at a time—longer if they handled groups during bow season too. But she also knew how much the guide services added to their income. People came from all over to ride into the wilderness and shoot an elk or deer. She wasn't really squeamish about the hunting. The herds needed to be managed, or they would overrun an area in just a few years. And most people ate what they killed. On the other hand, with the price they paid for a guided hunt, they could buy an entire side of beef.

Dad brushed a stray hair off her cheek, interrupting her thoughts. "We'll ride in Friday morning. Think you can manage around here for a week or two?"

She nodded and tried to smile. She knew Dad didn't like leaving her and Ryan any more than she liked having him gone. Sulking would only make it harder on both of them.

She picked up a cookie and tried to change the subject. "How was the cattle drive?"

Dad leaned back in his chair and stretched, working the kinks out of his muscles. "It went fine. But I'll tell you what, I'm getting too old to sleep on the ground." He grinned. "Even my toenails ache."

She wanted to say, "Then how are you going to manage a two-week scouting trip?" but she knew better than to bring up that subject again.

Dad looked at Colin. "No sign of that cougar; not even tracks. We lost one calf, though." He frowned. "It was still-born, but I'm not sure why. The heifer checks out okay."

A stiff wind rattled the shutters, and everyone watched as leaves and twigs blew across the yard. Greg got up and went over to the window, tipping his head to see the thermometer mounted on the deck post just outside. "Thirty degrees already. Good thing it's not wet; we'd have a hard freeze."

Colin joined him at the window. "I heard it's supposed to drop into the low twenties tonight. We'd better get the mammas and babies in the barn."

"I get to come!" Ryan stuffed the last of a snickerdoodle in his mouth and yanked on his father's shirtsleeve. "Tell them I can help. I want to see the calves."

Kara saw Greg roll his eyes, but he turned to face the window and didn't say anything. She smiled to herself. She couldn't blame him. Ryan could be a pest, and his "help" was guaranteed to slow down any chore.

Ryan shifted his pleading eyes to Colin.

"Hey, Sport, don't look at me. It's up to your dad."

Dad rubbed his chin and pretended to think about it, while Ryan hopped from one foot to the other and shouted, "Please, please, please?"

Kara covered her ears. "Ry! You're in the house."

She was glad when Dad gave up the game and consented. "Okay, as long as you mind Greg and Colin and stay out of the way, got it?"

"All right. I can go!"

Ryan made a mad dash for the door, where Anne stood holding out his heavy blue parka with the hood.

"You will need this, I think."

"Aw . . ." One look at Dad's face quieted any protest.

Greg and Colin grabbed their own coats from the rack on the service porch, pulled on gloves, and followed Ryan outside.

"Back in a few," Colin called.

"Yeah, hours." Greg pulled the door shut as a gust of icy wind blew the newspaper all over the room.

Kara sighed. She hadn't had a chance to talk to Colin about the field trip, but the quiet was comforting. She settled back in her chair and realized she felt more relaxed than she had in a week. It felt good to be with her family—back to the old routine.

A pang of loneliness gripped her as she thought about the one family member who wasn't there. *Mom would be standing at the window, watching to be sure Ryan didn't strip off his coat as soon as he thought he was out of sight. Then she would turn back to the table and offer Dad more coffee and say, "Do you have homework, Wakara?" Dad would kiss Mom on the cheek, ask "What's for dinner?", then take his paperwork into the den.*

"Wakara? Did you hear me?"

She snapped out of her dream. "Uh, sorry, Dad. What did you say?"

He must have read the sadness on her face, because he looked down and got busy folding the map. "I was reminding you that Wednesday is Greg's birthday." He looked up

48

again. "That's another reason we postponed the scouting trip. I thought we could celebrate Wednesday night."

Kara groaned. That's right! She had forgotten. Her brother would turn nineteen on Wednesday, and she hadn't even thought about a gift.

"Colin and I got him a GPS—a Global Positioning System. It works by locking onto satellites and pinpointing exactly where you are, anywhere in the world. You save your coordinates before a hike, and it will get you back within a hundred yards of where you started." Dad's eyes gleamed. "I bought myself one too. As much as we're in the woods, it's worth the cost."

"I've heard of them." She examined the device Dad had set on the table. "It looks like a remote control with a TV screen. Doesn't it work like a compass?"

Dad nodded. "Yes, but it actually stores positions. There's an instruction video that goes with it. If you don't mind, Sugar Bear, I thought we'd put your name on that."

She nodded, relieved. "Sure. I'll pick up a birthday card tomorrow."

Dad pulled out his wallet. "Here's your allowance and an extra fifteen dollars. Do you think you could get a cake too?"

"No need." Anne retrieved the plate of cookies and set them out of reach on the counter. "I will bake the cake. Chocolate with lemon filling."

Dad eyed the cookie plate. "Um, is that what he asked for?"

Anne shook her head. "No. But it is his favorite." A long, low moo sounded as she lifted the lid to the cow-shaped cookie jar and began filling it with what was left of the snickerdoodles. "Dinner is salmon," she said.

Kara stifled a giggle. Anne might as well have slapped Dad's hand. And she was right. Chocolate cake with lemon filling *was* Greg's favorite. "There are candles in the junk drawer," she told Anne, "and I saw some wrapping paper in the hall closet upstairs."

Dad watched the last cookie disappear into the jar, then pushed back from the table. "All right. Looks like you two have it under control." He gathered up the map and papers from the table, kissed the top of Kara's hair, and headed for his den.

6

BY WEDNESDAY NIGHT, the heifers with calves were penned inside the cowshed, while the rest of the herd grazed in the south pasture, where they could find shelter among scrub oak and ponderosa pines.

The bunkhouse walls were fully insulated and finished with a new coat of paint. The roof had been patched and the water pipes wrapped so they wouldn't freeze. Colin and Greg were all set to move back in after the birthday party, but Dad had other ideas.

"Colin, if you don't mind, I'd like you to stay in the house while Greg and I are gone."

He didn't say, "I don't want the women to be alone," but Kara knew that was the reason, and she felt a warm rush of gratitude. Not that she was afraid, but she liked it when everyone was together. It would be bad enough having Dad and Greg out in the middle of nowhere, let alone wondering if Colin was okay out in the bunkhouse by himself. Besides, Ryan enjoyed the male company.

"All right!" Ryan proved her thoughts by spraying mashed potatoes all over his placemat.

"Ryan Sheridan, not with your mouth full!" She handed him a napkin and watched him dab at a couple splotches of gravy.

He swallowed and wiped his mouth with the same napkin, spreading the white-and-brown mixture across his cheek and chin. "Colin likes my room. The bed is more comfortable, huh, Colin?"

Colin stopped with a fork full of peas halfway to his mouth. "Uh, sure, Partner. I'll be happy to keep you company."

Ryan giggled at the John Wayne accent. Kara rolled her eyes and went back to cutting her roast beef. Anne had gone all out for Greg's birthday, adding rolls with real butter to his favorite meal.

After dinner, Anne shooed them all out of the kitchen and into the living room. "Time for presents," she said. "We will clean later."

Kara tried to ignore the tingle she felt when Colin sat next to her on the couch. They'd both been so busy lately, they'd hardly had time to say hello to each other. He hadn't mentioned last Friday night, or offered to go with her to this week's game. And she still hadn't asked him about the survival class.

Greg sat in the middle of the floor to open his gifts. That had been a tradition in their family ever since she could remember.

Colin was as excited over the GPS as Greg was. He even squeezed her hand when Greg opened the instruction video. "Whew, I thought we were going to have to read some hulking manual to learn how to work that thing," he laughed.

"Yeah. This will make it a lot easier," Greg agreed. "Thanks, Sis."

Greg's smile as he looked at Kara was genuine. It made her feel warm all over to see him acting normal again. After their mom's death, it was like her brother had an evil twin who took his place. Now the bad twin had finally disappeared, and her real brother was back. She hoped it was for good.

Ryan handed him a wad of comic book paper rolled in scotch tape. Greg laughed, then hugged him when he opened it and found a waterproof case with at least a hundred matches.

Anne's gift was a long bundle rolled in tissue paper and tied with string. Everyone gasped when Greg carefully unrolled the new saddle blanket out onto the carpet. He traced the intricate red-and-black pattern with his finger. "You made this, didn't you?"

Kara knew it was true. When Anne had come back from Idaho, she had brought her loom with her and set it up in a corner of the family room. Kara had often seen her working on the blanket but promised not to say anything. Anne was always careful to put everything away before the men came in, and Kara had kept the secret.

Greg was still studying his gift. "Thank you, Anne. I-I don't know what to say. It's awesome."

The cook's eyes softened. "A warm blanket is good for the outside of horse, and man."

When Anne left the room to get the cake, Kara was sure she saw tears in her older brother's eyes.

After eating a small piece of cake, Kara excused herself and ran upstairs to finish her homework, but the words on the pages of her history book blurred as she wiped away her own tears. Would there ever be an end to the crying?

She picked up her Bible and found the list of verses the pastor had quoted at her mother's funeral. She found the one she was looking for at the bottom of the page. "Weep-

53

ing may last for the night, but joy comes in the morning." Did that mean she would someday think about her mother with joy instead of sadness?

It had already been over a year. And if she were honest, they had all come a long way. Greg was staying out of trouble. Ryan came to her or Anne when he needed something, and that desperate look less and less often clouded her father's eyes.

"What about me, Lord?" she whispered. "Will I ever be able to forget her?"

She knew the answer to that. *Never!* But if these verses were true, and she believed they were, someday she would have only happy memories. She sighed and slipped the worn piece of notebook paper back into the pages of her Bible. At least her nightmares had stopped, she realized with a shock. They had been terrifying—she and Mom running from the car wreck through a raging fire, becoming separated in the thick, smothering smoke. Kara always made it out, but Mom never did.

"You would think being trapped by a forest fire would have made the dreams worse," she told Tia later on the phone. "But I haven't had one since we came home."

"Too weird," Tia agreed.

After they hung up, Kara went downstairs to say goodnight and maybe talk Anne into a second piece of cake.

Everyone was gathered at the kitchen table. Ryan was busy slurping up a second bowl of ice cream, while the others once again bent over the map. Colin smiled as she took the empty seat next to her father. Anne set a bowl of ice cream in front of her.

Suddenly she didn't feel very hungry.

"Colin will go with us as far as Pinewood Meadow, so he can bring the truck and trailer back," Dad said.

He turned to Greg. "When's Mark bringing in the radio?"

"Monday morning."

Kara tried to push aside a new wave of fear. Since the fire, she sometimes felt afraid for no real reason. Her hands got sweaty, and her chest felt so heavy she had to concentrate to breathe. She felt like that now. Dad and Greg would be there three whole days without a radio. What would they do if something happened and they needed help?

"What's the weather report?" Greg asked.

Dad's voice sounded far away. "Cold and clear through Sunday. After that, it's anybody's guess."

Kara kept her head down. Her hands were still shaking, but she was breathing better, and the feeling of panic was starting to pass.

Anne's hand squeezed her shoulder as she handed her a cup of hot tea. Kara picked out the scent of chamomile with a touch of lavender. One of Anne's special brews. She tried to say thank you, but the words wouldn't come.

"What's wrong with Kara?"

Ryan's loud question brought her head up. Everyone was staring. All she wanted to do was escape to her room. She tried to push back from the table, but her body had a different idea. It was like she was glued to the chair. *Oh, God, please don't let me faint again!* This was so embarrassing! What was wrong with her?

Dad laid a hand against her forehead. "No fever."

Once again, Anne came to her rescue. "It is too hot in here, I think."

Dad took his hand away but kept an eye on her as he folded the map and handed it to Greg. "Put this with the rest of the equipment. Then you and Colin better get some sleep. We've got a lot to do tomorrow." His tone was polite but sharp. Colin and Greg jumped up and took off without a word.

"You too, Tiger."

Ryan scowled. "Why?"

"Get ready for bed." Dad's tone softened. "I'll be up before you go to sleep."

Anne helped Ryan out of his chair and took his hand. "Come. You will pick out a story."

Ryan scuffed his feet but went with Anne. Wakara wanted to follow them, but Dad's look told her to stay.

When the door swung shut behind them, he cleared his throat. "Okay, Sugar Bear, what's going on?"

She didn't know what to say. How could she tell him everything she was feeling when she didn't understand it herself?

"Are things okay at school?"

She nodded. "Fine."

He sighed and began to study the inside of his coffee cup. She hated it when he got that wounded look. The last time she'd seen it was when Greg was in trouble. Now she was the one causing Dad pain, and that was the last thing she wanted.

"I'm sorry. I didn't mean to break up your meeting."

He looked up sharply. "You didn't break up anything, Wakara. I sent the boys away because I know something is bothering you, and I don't want to go away without at least trying to help."

Her throat tightened. If this were Mom, she'd tell her how scared she was, and they'd both have a good cry. But Mom wasn't here. And Dad was leaving.

She had known for weeks that he'd be taking this trip, and she had dreaded it so much she'd pretended it wouldn't happen. Now he was going, and she couldn't do anything about it.

"I don't think you should go." There, she'd said it. Now what?

Dad frowned. "Into Cutter's Gap? Why?"

Why? It was so obvious, how could he miss it! She didn't try to stop the irritation in her voice. "Dad! Look at how

56

cold it is already. You said yourself no one can hunt in there this year, so what makes you think it's safe to scout?" She knew she sounded disrespectful, but she couldn't seem to stop herself.

"You won't even have a radio until Monday. And if it's too cloudy, Mark might not even be able to make it in. And what about the horses? The hay there is worthless from all that smoke, and there can't be any grass left." Her eyes were tearing up, but she was too mad to care. "I was there. I know. That fire was so hot, nothing could have survived. All the animals were either roasted or they ran away. The elk are probably all in Alaska by now!" She stood up, amazed to hear herself practically shouting. "You can ground me for a year, but I don't want you to go!"

Dad looked like she'd just hit him with a brick. She wanted to stalk out of the room, but his eyes wouldn't let her.

He opened his mouth, then closed it again and buried his face in his hands.

Her defiance melted. She wanted to run into his arms like she had as a little girl, back when a hug was enough to make the hurt go away. "Dad, I'm sorry. I don't know why I said all that. Please don't cry."

He lifted his head and ran a hand across his eyes. Kara couldn't believe it—tears were running down his cheeks all right, but he was actually laughing!

"Wakara Windsong Sheridan," he said when he could talk again, "you sound just like your mother!"

7

ON FRIDAY MORNING, Wakara's alarm went off at 6 A.M. She hit the snooze button and rolled over, burrowing under the covers. She had another ten minutes before she had to wake Ryan and crawl into the shower. Suddenly she was wide awake. Dad and Greg were leaving today! She tugged on sweatpants and the oversized flannel shirt that served as her bathrobe and hurried into the bathroom. The mirror reflected blotchy skin and red-rimmed eyes.

Last night, she'd finally asked Colin if he would help her put together a presentation for the field trip. He'd said "Sure!" right away, and she had stayed up until two going over the manual Mr. Jaminson had given her. There was only one copy, and Colin would have to read it when she was through.

She washed her face, brushed her teeth, and quickly braided her hair. The shower could wait until after Dad was gone.

She found Ryan in the kitchen wolfing down cold cereal and a thick slice of Anne's whole wheat toast dripping with strawberry jam. Dad stood on the service porch, pushing his arms into the sleeves of a thick, blue parka. Outside, a horse whinnied, and someone clucked gently, coaxing it into the trailer.

"We're taking Buck and Chief, and one mule." Dad slipped an arm around her shoulder.

She had wondered which horses they would ride. Both of these were Appaloosas—big, strong, and even more stubborn than the pack mule, but they were surefooted and spook-proof. She nodded. "Good choice. They can handle that rugged terrain."

She looked up to see Dad's teasing smile. "Well, I'm glad you approve." He hugged her hard and kissed the top of her head.

He ruffled Ryan's hair before doing the same to him. "Be good, okay?"

Ryan glared into his cereal bowl. "Do I hafta mind Kara?"

"Yes, you have to mind your sister. Anne too. And I'm counting on you to go easy on them."

"Can I ride Star?"

"Only if someone has time to go with you." He cupped Ryan's chin in his hand. "And don't drive them crazy asking, got it?"

"I won't." He hesitated, then said, "Dad?"

"What is it, Tiger?"

"Come home, okay?"

Dad closed his eyes, and the pain on his face made Kara want to cry. Sometimes she forgot that Ryan must be scared of losing Dad too, like they had lost Mom. She knew, though, that their fear only made Dad's job harder.

She crossed the kitchen and gave Ryan's shoulders a gentle squeeze. "Come on, Ry. Time for school. And if it doesn't rain this afternoon, we'll take Star and Lily into the pasture and practice rounding up cows." She knew she would probably regret that promise, but it was worth it just to see her little brother's bright smile.

Wakara watched until the truck and trailer pulled out of the drive, then realized they had missed the school bus. Tia's mom came to the rescue again and dropped them all off at school. "You're on your own this afternoon, though," she warned. "I've got a late meeting."

"No prob." Tia kissed her mother on the cheek. "Wakara and I have to do some research on the computer, so I'll be at her house for awhile."

Kara groaned inwardly. She had forgotten she'd promised Tia they would do another search on the web this afternoon. That paper on the Yahi-Yana Indians was due in three weeks.

She was excited about Tia's project. In her heart she had this dream that their research would prove once and for all who her true ancestors were. But she also had to put together supplies for the survival demonstration. The field trip was scheduled for next Monday, and she and Colin planned to do a trial run tomorrow afternoon. Even without the ride she had promised Ryan, she would be up again until midnight.

"You'll have to go home afterward and get Patches," she told Tia as they headed for the lockers. "I promised Ryan we would ride."

It was Tia's turn to groan. "Aiiya! Major pain!"

Kara grinned. "Come on, be a sport. Maybe Ry will turn out to be a good partner for calf roping."

"In my worst nightmare!" Tia squealed.

The first bell echoed through the hallway. Kara grabbed her History notebook and headed to her least favorite class of the day.

The bus ride home seemed to take forever. By the time she changed clothes, brushed down the horses, and gave Ryan a lesson in saddling Star, it was after five o'clock. The light was fading from the western sky.

60

"Hurry, Kara. It's getting dark already!"

"Don't worry," she said, "we've still got a good half hour." *Please,* she prayed silently. She gave Ryan a leg up, then mounted Lily. Tia and Patches were already loping around the perimeter of the pasture. "Ground's soft," Tia yelled as she rode by.

Wakara urged Lily forward at a gentle walk, Star right on their heels. He was a trail horse in the summer and used to riding nose to tail. Kara could tell right away that Lily wasn't pleased with that arrangement. The mare nickered and danced, then kicked out.

Ryan yelled, "Hey! Cut it out. You're gonna hurt my horse."

She had no idea what happened next. She had just turned Lily's nose so they could ride side by side when Star jumped like he'd been stung by a bee and took off across the pasture.

"Hang on!" Kara screamed, but Ryan was already bent over the pony's neck and hanging on for dear life.

Cows scattered everywhere as the frightened pony tore across the pasture. Kara had never seen him move that fast. She kicked Lily and sent her into a dead run. Tia and Patches were riding hard from the opposite direction. If they could get Star between them, he would probably calm down.

But the pony evaded capture by spinning around and heading the other direction at breakneck speed. Kara couldn't believe Ryan was still hanging on. His face, as the pony raced past them, was white as a sheet.

Lily and Patches spun in unison, split one to each side, and herded Star toward the round pen by the barn.

They almost made it.

Lily's gait changed as they reached the softer, muck-covered ground. "Ryan, bale out!" Kara yelled, but she knew he never would. She hadn't taught him yet how to jump, tuck his head, and roll away from the horse.

The soft, hoof-sucking mud must have been too much for Star. The pony never even slowed. He just stopped. Kara watched in horror as her little brother flew out of the saddle, over the horse's head, and landed with a sloshing sound in a mound of manure-soaked muck.

She didn't remember what happened next. But Tia was more than happy to spread the news to everyone in the county.

"Wakara lost it, I swear!" she told Colin and Anne later. "Lily would have stopped, but Wakara bailed out anyway and rolled right up next to Ryan. When he saw her, he started kicking and screaming at her to leave him alone, and she, like, picked up this whole handful of horse poop and, splat, dumped it right on top of his head."

Kara didn't remember doing that, but it must have worked, because Ryan quit fighting her, jumped up, and ran for the barn. She hadn't heard the truck pull in either, but she caught up with Ry just as Colin came rushing in from the other direction. He grabbed Ryan's shoulders and held him still while they checked for sprains or broken bones.

"He's all right," she said when he finally quieted down.

Colin released Ryan, then looked at her and started laughing. "Well, Miss Kara, looks like you take first prize."

She peeled off her filthy jacket and tossed it, along with her gloves, into a bucket by the tack room. "First prize in what?"

"Why, mud wrestling, Ma'am." He tipped his hat, then stood and turned Ryan around. Ryan's face and hair were caked with muck except for under his eyes, where tears had diluted the mixture enough for his skin to show through.

"Sorry, Princess," Colin said, "but you look even worse than he does."

Anne met them on the porch. Wakara had never seen her rattled before, but the cook's face was as white as Ryan's had been. When Kara and Colin assured her everyone was all right, she swung her cast around and sat down heavily on the bench. Ryan burst into tears again and ran into her arms.

"That stupid, snot-face Star. I don't like him anymore."

Anne held him a minute, then pushed him to arm's length. "To learn to ride, you must learn to fall."

She looked at Wakara. "For now, you must get warm."

Only then did Kara realize she was shaking, and her fingers, without the gloves, were prickly with cold.

Colin took Ryan's hand and led him toward the bunkhouse, where they had just installed a second shower. "Come on, cowboy, let's get you cleaned up."

Tia flashed Wakara a sympathetic look. "You'd better go in. I'll take care of the horses."

Kara nodded gratefully and followed Anne into the house. She stripped off her shirt and jeans, tossed them into the stationary tub by the washer, and hurried upstairs.

Twenty minutes later, she had showered and finished drying her hair. She picked through the nearly empty closet, then pulled on clean jeans and the soft, blue turtleneck Dad had given her last Christmas. She felt a slight thrill when she thought about tomorrow's plans with Colin. Working out the survival routine for Health class would be fun.

The smell that greeted her when she opened her bedroom door made her mouth water. She took the stairs two at a time and made it to the kitchen just as Tia walked in the back door.

"The horses are in their stalls. I hosed off their legs and gave them some grain, but Star was so tired, he just lay down." She paused and sniffed. "Umm, what's that smell?"

Kara lifted the lid on a huge cast-iron skillet sitting on the back of the stove. "It's Anne's beef Stroganoff." She grinned at Tia. "I'll check on Star after dinner. Want to stay?"

Tia dove for the phone. "I'll call Pops and tell him I'll be late. We haven't even started on our homework."

8

"OH, MY GOODNESS, they found Ishi's brain!"

"What?" Kara set aside her history book and joined Tia at the computer. "Where? What do you mean, 'they found Ishi's brain'?"

"Only in the Smithsonian! Look—it says in this article Ishi's brain has been in storage for eighty-two years, and now some tribes in northern California want it back. This is too weird."

Kara felt a surge of excitement. There was less than a zero chance this Ishi was her relative, but because his mother's nickname was Wakara, she somehow felt a kinship to both of them.

It was a long article. Kara pulled each page from the printer as soon as it came out and stacked the pages in chronological order.

"Whoa. You're right. It says here that historical records document the Yana survivors who found refuge among other tribes."

Tia broke in, "Right. Ishi was Yahi, but they were an off-shoot from the Yana tribe, and the languages were really close. That means the word *Wakara* could have come from either group."

"And there are descendants of the Yana tribe still there." Wakara felt goose bumps up and down her arms.

"Yeah." Tia scrolled back to the first page. When it was on the screen, she drew the mouse along one sentence and clicked on the BOLD key. "Here—the Redding Rancheria and Pit River Tribe."

"I see that." Kara scanned the pages. "But what I don't get is how Ishi's brain got to the Smithsonian Institution in the first place."

Tia scrolled to page two of the report. "Remember Theodora Kroeber, the lady who wrote that book?"

"Sure."

"It says here that her husband was the head anthropologist at the University of California when Ishi was found. He's the one who sent Ishi's brain to the Smithsonian in 1917. Eewww, gross! They lost it or packed it away or something. Now they're going to send it back."

"Correction. Look at the date on this, Tia. Page one. They already sent it back."

Tia scrolled back to the beginning of the report. "April 1999. Wow. Last year! You're right, that means it should be a done deal. Ishi's brain and the rest of him are probably reburied by now.

"This is too cool. Am I going to get an A on this project, or what?" Tia jumped to her feet and grabbed the papers Kara had stacked on the end of her bed.

"Anne's got to see this. Do you think she's still in the kitchen? I could use another piece of Greg's birthday cake."

Kara laughed. "Tia, you're amazing. How can you eat so many sweets and not get sick? Chocolate before bed gives me weird dreams."

Tia grinned. "Mom says I've got a great metabolism. Pops says I was born with an iron gut—whatever that's supposed to mean. Either way, I'm not complaining."

"All right. But I'll get the cake. Anne is in the family room, and we're not supposed to disturb her unless it's really important."

"How can you say this isn't important? They're your ancestors!"

"And most of them have been dead for nearly a hundred years," Kara said as she threw an arm around her friend's shoulder and led her to the bedroom door. "If you want cake, we'd better get it now. Your dad will be here in ten minutes."

Kara had a glass of milk, while Tia polished off a huge slice of birthday cake. When a horn honked in the driveway, she walked her friend to the porch and waved good-bye. She watched until the taillights on Tia's father's pickup disappeared around the corner, then leaned against the porch rail and looked up. It was cold and clear, with no moon, and the sky was studded with at least a zillion stars.

Diamonds on black velvet. That's what Mom always called them. *Look, Wakara, have you ever seen anything more beautiful? Just try and count those stars, then remember God's blessings are more numerous than the sky can hold.*

Kara hugged herself and closed her eyes. She could almost feel Mom's arm slip around her, warming her shoulders. *I love you, Wakara.* The words flashed through her mind as if someone had actually spoken.

She shivered and gazed once more into the sparkling sky. "I love you too, God," she whispered. "And Mom too. Please tell her for me, okay?"

Suddenly she realized her feet were freezing. Even thick, wool socks and a heavy sweatshirt weren't enough protection for a night like this.

66

She closed the door quietly behind her, turned the latch, and then hung her sweatshirt on the rack in the entryway. She was halfway across the living room before she noticed Colin watching her from the bottom of the stairs. "Whoa! You scared me. How long have you been there?"

Colin grinned. "Sorry. It's after nine o'clock. You've been out there for awhile, so I was just coming down to see if you were all right."

Kara didn't know if she should feel irritated or pleased that he was keeping track of her. She decided it didn't matter. "I was just coming up to check on Ryan."

"He's out for the count," Colin chuckled. "I couldn't even interest him in a second piece of cake. Too much excitement for one day, I guess."

Kara felt a flash of guilt. Ryan had been quiet at dinner, but she and Tia had been so caught up in their own conversation, she'd forgotten to ask if he'd recovered from his fall.

"Is he okay?" she asked Colin now. "Does he have many bruises?"

"Nah. Just a sore bottom from bouncing around so much. That pony saddle isn't padded." He laughed out loud, then shook his head. "Sorry, I know it's not funny, but I'd bet that old horse hasn't ever moved so fast in his life. He's probably twice as sore as Ryan."

Kara slapped her forehead with the palm of her hand. "Oh, no! Tia said Star was pretty stiff. I meant to go back out there and forgot."

"Don't worry about it. I rubbed him down and gave him a dose of Banamine. He'll be fine in the morning."

"Thanks." She laid her hand against his arm. "I owe you one. No, two. You took care of Ryan while I was goofing around with Tia. I'm sorry, Colin. That's not your job."

"Hey." His head snapped up. "Don't be so hard on yourself." He drew his arm away and turned to face her, the look in his eyes both wistful and sad. "And please don't say it's not my job, okay? I like to think I'm part of this family too."

He stepped aside and motioned her up the stairs. "I'll get the lights. You'd better get some rest. We've got a lot to do tomorrow."

His grin was back, and she felt a thrill of excitement. Tomorrow they would collect the final equipment and do a test run for the survival class. She started to tell him "Thanks," but he was already through the kitchen doorway and out of sight.

Is Colin part of the family? She thought about it as she went upstairs, brushed her teeth, and headed to her room. He'd only been around since June. And yet, so had Anne, and she had definitely become a part of the Sheridan clan. Did that mean she had to treat Colin like a brother? Worse yet, did he think of her as a sister?

The thought made her chest ache. *Knock it off, Wako.* She propped up two pillows and plopped down on the bed. Colin might be part of the family, but he wasn't a blood brother. Nothing could change that. And nothing could change the strange way she felt when he was around. Sometimes life was so confusing. She closed her eyes. "Oh, Mom," she whispered, "I sure wish you were here. Who am I supposed to talk to about this stuff?"

She looked at the clock. It was after ten, her brain felt like a bowl of mush, and she still didn't have her homework done.

She went back to her history lesson, but the stack of computer printouts kept drawing her attention away from the Civil War. After reading one paragraph three times, she gave up and closed the book.

She scanned the stack of papers. A few of Ishi's blood relatives might have joined some of the other tribes in the area, but what difference did that make to her? Her great-grandmother had been found near a Nez Perce reservation. And the Nez Perce were nowhere near California.

Kara sighed and laid the papers on her desk, then shut down the computer. All this stuff about Ishi and his brain might be great for Tia's report, but as far as she was concerned, it just added more pieces to a very frustrating puzzle.

9

THUD! THUMP! The pounding sound interrupted a pleasant dream. She'd been riding bareback, cantering across an open meadow, the warm wind tossing her hair around her face and shoulders. She could feel the horse's muscles bulge, then extend, as strong legs churned through a sea of springtime grass. Never before had she felt so weightless and free.

Wakara rolled over and stretched. She shoved the covers away from her face and propped herself up on her elbows.

"What?" Her question sounded as groggy as she felt.

The door flew open and a skinny, flannel-draped body bounced onto the foot of her bed.

She sat up straighter, glanced at the clock, and groaned. "Ryan Sheridan, it's seven o'clock on a Saturday morning. You'd better have a good excuse for waking me up."

He leaned forward and peered into her eyes. "You awake, Kara? Cuz Colin said to get up and come downstairs, he wants to get going."

"Oh, yeah? Well, tell His Majesty I'll be there in a few minutes." She yawned and flopped down on her pillow, but Ryan tugged on her arm.

"What's a majesty?" Ryan went on before she could answer. "Colin said don't let you go back to sleep. Anne's making waffles, and I got to get my survival kit so you can borrow it for your class."

She gave up and flung her legs over the edge of the bed. "There, are you satisfied?" She ruffled his prickly scalp. "Now, go tell Colin I'll be right down, okay?"

"Okay, but first I gotta get my bag." He scrambled off the bed and out the door without shutting it behind him.

Kara looked longingly at her pillow, then pushed her feet into the fur-lined slippers she'd gotten last Christmas from Aunt Peg. She'd almost exchanged them for a pair of unlined moccasins, but now she was glad she hadn't. The leather soles and llama-wool lining kept her feet and ankles warm even on cold winter mornings.

"Brrr!" She grabbed her red flannel shirt and tugged it on over her cotton pajamas. *It might as well be winter,* she thought as she headed for the bathroom, *but it's only the end of September.* She brushed her teeth, pulled on jeans and a turtleneck shirt, then topped it with a knee-length wool sweater.

Downstairs she found Ryan, Colin, and Anne in the kitchen. "What is with this weather?" She rubbed a clear spot on the steam-clouded glass and peered out the window. Ice crystals made weblike patterns around the outside of the pane, and the few leaves that still dangled from the oak tree were rimmed with white.

"Winter Warrior visits in the night." Anne set a plate of steaming waffles on the table.

Kara pulled out her chair and sat down next to Ryan, who was licking syrup-coated peanut butter off his knife. "Nuh-uh," he said. "It was Jack Frost. Colin said."

71

Anne smiled. "Among my people it is said that when the leaves turn brown and Mother Earth begins to sing her death song, Angel Maiden mourns for her. Winter Warrior collects Angel Maiden's tears and pours them on Mother Earth. Each leaf, seed, and blade of grass is wrapped in a blanket of ice, until the time of new birth. Then Angel Maiden's tears turn to rain, melt the ice, and new life is born from the frozen ground."

Ryan scowled. "Then who's Jack Frost?"

Anne turned away from the table, and Kara bit her lip to keep from laughing. She flashed Colin a look that clearly said, "How are you going to get out of this one?"

Colin cleared his throat, thought a minute, then said seriously, "Well, it's like this. Your sister's name is Wakara, right?"

Ryan's scowl deepened. "Yeah."

"But some people call her Kara."

Ryan nodded.

Colin pointed to Kara, then to the kitchen window. "Kara is Wakara's nickname and Jack Frost is a nickname for Winter Warrior. Get it?"

Ryan looked at Anne for confirmation, but the cook was bent over the sink, intent on scouring the bacon pan. From where she was sitting, Wakara could see Anne's mouth twitching in silent laughter. When Ryan turned his head in her direction, Kara grabbed her fork and got busy with her breakfast.

He must have taken their silence for agreement. "Oh. I get it." He shoveled the last two bites of waffle into his mouth, pushed his plate aside, and reached under his chair.

"Here's my survival bag." He handed it to Colin. "But you can only borrow it. I need to keep it under my bed in case of emergency."

"Thanks. I promise we'll take good care of it."

Kara could feel Colin staring at her. She finally looked up.

72

"Are you about ready, Wakara? Winter Warrior hasn't done us any favors, but at least the training will be more realistic."

His eyes dared her to laugh. She almost choked trying not to. She nodded, washed down the last bite of waffle with a swallow of coffee, and pushed to her feet. "I gathered some supplies. They're in my backpack. Do you have the manual?"

"Right there." Colin pointed to his own backpack propped in the corner by the coatrack, right next to her dad's tool kit and a ball of thick twine.

She paused. "What's with the tools?"

He stood and flexed his arms, rolled his shoulders, and did some deep side bends. Kara flinched when she saw the pain flash across his face.

He must have seen her concern. "Just limbering up."

He moved past her to the coatrack and grabbed a thick, brown parka off the hook. "And to answer your question, we need the tools because we're going to build a travois."

Ryan's head snapped up. "What's a travois?"

"A cart without wheels. You pull it with ropes or strap it behind a horse." Kara stared at Colin. "Why do we need a travois?"

Anne spoke up. "It is a way to carry those who cannot walk, especially over snow."

Ryan's eyes widened. "Like the toboggan they use when they rescue people from avalanches and stuff?"

"Not exactly," Kara broke in. But Ryan was too excited to listen.

"They wrap them all up, tie them in, and ski down the mountain. Can I help? I'll be the hurt guy."

"Not this time, Sport." Colin grinned at Wakara. "A travois is also good for carrying wood. I thought we'd take advantage of the trip into the woods and clean up some of the debris along the trail. Anne can use the smaller pieces for kindling."

73

"The trail? I thought we were going to practice in the pasture?" Kara felt a chill even through her sweater. She hadn't been on the trail through the woods since the Carlson boys chased off that cougar, and she wasn't sure she wanted to go back again so soon.

Colin wrinkled his nose. "For what we're going to do, I'd rather avoid the mud." He grinned. "Besides, cow pies are great for building a fire if they're dry, but they're no good to us frozen."

She couldn't argue with that. Still, she hadn't counted on venturing into those woods this soon. What if the big cat was still around? Worse, what if Lily was still spooked and wouldn't go? *Cut it out, Wako—if you're nervous, Lily will feel it for sure.*

She gathered up her dishes and carried them to the sink. Anne nodded her thanks, then whispered so that only Kara could hear, "God has not given you a spirit of fear."

Where had that come from? She spotted Anne's Bible on the counter next to the telephone. That's right, it was part of a verse in 1 Timothy. She had probably read it a dozen times, but she couldn't remember the rest. She'd have to look it up later. Right now, Colin was waiting for her.

By the time she gathered her stuff and met him in the barn, Colin was busy on his project. While he finished nailing boards together, she pulled items out of the backpacks and went over the checklist.

"First aid kit, waterproof matches, space blanket." She checked space blanket off the list. "We should carry two of these. In this kind of weather one wouldn't be enough."

"Good thinking." He put the hammer away and came over to stand beside her. "What about a signal mirror?"

"I thought we'd use Ryan's. If we don't use something from his bag, we'll hurt his feelings."

"Safety pins, canteen, knife, flashlight, bouillon cubes, salt . . ." He shuffled things around. "Looks like everything's here."

"Not quite." She handed him a plastic bag. "Candy bars, dried fruit sticks, and beef jerky. You can't live off berries this time of year."

Colin's eyes lit up. "Way to go, Wakara."

She laughed. "You sound like Tia."

Dakota nickered and pawed the ground, signaling that he, at least, was ready to go. Colin reached through the stall door and rubbed the gelding's nose. "Hang on, boy, we've got a lot to pack."

"You said that right." Kara picked up a hatchet and a small folding saw. "Most people would never carry around all this stuff."

She thought back to her and Ryan's escape from the forest fire. They had nothing with them then except canteens, their jackets, and Ryan's simple survival kit. With God's help, that had been enough.

Colin must have been thinking along the same lines. "During the fire, Anne and I didn't have anything except her fishing gear. And that was no help at all. In a real emergency, you usually have to make do with whatever's at hand."

She nodded. "True, but if anyone's going camping, hiking, or horseback riding, they should know what to take along." She thought a minute. "Maybe we can show them some of both."

Colin knelt down and began dividing the items into two piles, one for each pack. "What do you mean?"

Kara sprinted into the tack room and came back with two sets of saddlebags. "We take it all: one-man tent, bedrolls, cord, coffee can, an aluminum pan—everything you need for a backpacking trip. The camping stuff goes on the horses, the rest goes in our packs. Then, when we've shown

75

them what to bring and how to pack it, we can demonstrate what to do if they're lost or caught out without their supplies."

"Whoa! Hold on. We've only got three hours, remember? I wanted to show them how to use a GPS."

She rolled her eyes. "Get serious. You watched the video and still don't have a clue how to use one."

Colin grinned, and she realized he was joking about the GPS.

"Look," she said, "this really won't take that long. They've got the supply list and pictures right in the book. We demonstrate how to use some of the stuff, then let them help with a project."

Colin sat back on his heels. "Just what project did you have in mind?"

She ignored his amused tone. "A pole shelter. Simple to build, and you can find materials in the woods in any kind of weather."

Colin just stared at her. "And what do they use for a cover?"

"A space blanket. One of the main pieces of survival equipment, remember?" She bent down and poked him in the chest. "Then, Mr. Sarcastic, we let them practice building a windbreak for the fire."

Colin toppled sideways, clutching at his heart. "Someone save me—she's not a teacher, she's a slave driver."

Kara ignored him. "I'll get the horses, you pack the bags."

By the time she had Lily brushed and saddled, Colin had all the supplies ready to load. He tied the saddlebags to the horses and slid open the barn door. The blast of cold air made her gasp. "Whoa, it hasn't warmed up any, has it?" She led Lily to the mounting block. It was just an old tree stump, but it was the perfect height.

Tia always teased her about having the shortest legs at Lariat High. It was true. She sometimes had a problem if she had to dismount on a trail, but she never rode that far alone, so someone was usually around to give her a leg up.

Colin had fashioned a travois from a piece of flat wood enclosed on three sides with lodgepole rails. He attached leather straps to the open end, strung them through guides over Dakota's rump, and tied them to the saddle. Dakota danced a bit and stamped his foot, but otherwise tolerated the contraption. Colin set both backpacks in the makeshift sled. "The weight will keep it from bouncing around. But we'll have to carry them back if we're toting wood."

"Fine by me, but you won't get much in that thing."

He tightened his horse's girth, then swung into the saddle. "Don't have to. All Anne wants is some kindling and a few pieces of juniper. She said to make sure the pieces still have bark and leaves." He wrinkled his nose. "She probably wants it for one of her brews. Remind me to never get sick."

Kara laughed. "Hey, some of that herbal stuff really works. Oh, I forgot." She dug two Ziploc bags out of her jacket pocket. "Anne sent these."

Colin clucked to Dakota and urged him forward. "Hot dogs! Anne thinks of everything."

Anne thinks of everything. How annoying! While she came up with the plans for their survival demonstration and gathered most of the supplies, Colin had stood there looking smug and questioned her ideas. But let Anne provide a package of wieners, and suddenly she's the world's greatest hero.

10

IT TOOK TWO HOURS TO REACH the clearing by the creek where they planned to practice. The trail was damp, most of it shaded by tall ponderosa pines, and the ground was still slick. Spider webs glistened like spun sugar between the frosted branches of the trees. The horses picked their way carefully, hooves crunching through the thin ice. They made several stops to clear away fallen limbs and line them up along the edges of the trail. The guys would come in later with a chain saw and cut the limbs into firewood.

Juniper was scarce and scattered among the larger trees. They had to go into the woods to gather what they needed, and Kara made sure she kept the trail in sight. She wasn't usually nervous in the woods, but with a big cat in the neighborhood, she couldn't help looking over her shoulder each time a twig snapped. Colin worked quietly. He kept his head up as he studied the tree line and peered behind large fallen logs.

They stacked most of the juniper and smaller pieces of wood by the trail to pick up on the way back, but Colin piled enough in the travois to build a fire for their midday meal.

While they were scavenging, they found several small branches from a lodgepole pine. Kara dragged them to the travois. "These will be great for the shelter."

Colin nodded and pointed to the curve up ahead. "Hear the water? We're almost there."

She slapped her gloved hands against her thighs. "Good. It's cold out here, and I'm already hungry."

He cupped his hands, fingers entwined, to give her a leg up into the saddle. "Let's go, Princess. I could eat a bite or two myself."

She hated it when he called her Princess, but she didn't object out loud—it was the nicest thing he had said to her all day. Actually, all week. They had hardly had any time together since the football game, and neither of them had even talked about going to last night's game in Lariat. She wondered if he would offer to come to the youth group meeting on Sunday night. *Should I invite him?* She really didn't know what to do. Colin had been acting strange ever since the fire. At the lodge, she was sure that he liked her as more than just a friend. Now it seemed like he was treating her more like a sister.

Lily picked up the scent of running water and hurried forward. Kara let her have her head, and the pretty mare practically pranced toward the creek. She dismounted and let Lily quench her thirst, then tied her reins around a sturdy tree. Colin came into the clearing more slowly. He had to keep the big gelding at a walk, or the makeshift travois would fall apart. Kara had to admit the device came in handy. Maybe when they got back she could help him make a better one.

They wasted no time building a fire. Kara scattered some dry moss in a small circle, then stacked kindling tepee-style inside the ring of blackened rocks, while Colin brought over some slightly bigger pieces from the travois. Her family had used this fire ring ever since she could remember.

"Is this your property or Carlsons'?" Colin stacked a piece of rotted Douglas fir on the small pile at his feet, then hunkered down to light the kindling that Kara had prepared. "Hey, good job."

Wakara felt a stab of irritation. Did he think she'd never done this before? She'd been building fires since she was Ryan's age. She sat back on her heels and watched him guide a lighted match between the twigs. *And,* she thought, *starting them with flint and steel since I was ten.*

Sometimes she forgot he'd only been around for about five months. He really didn't know much about her. She wondered how much Greg had told him—probably not much. She and Greg were too far apart in age to be close friends. She doubted he even thought about her very much, let alone talked about her to his buddies.

Colin had opened up to her a little back when he first came to the ranch, then again this summer when they were at Eagle Lodge. He had told her that his parents were divorced, that he'd spent some time in a youth camp for troubled teens, then he'd finally gone to live with his uncle in Alaska. That was where he had learned about woodsmanship and horses.

"Wakara?"

"Sorry. You wanted to know about the boundaries." She plopped down with her legs crossed Indian style and held her hands over the flickering flame. "This clearing is actually on both properties. I don't think anyone really knows where the line is. In fact, the entire trail crosses over so many times we don't even try to figure it out."

Colin carefully crossed two small pieces of wood on top of the now steadily burning kindling and huddled close, holding out his hands and rubbing them together.

Small fire—get close—stay warm. Big fire—stay back—get cold. She couldn't remember where she'd learned that, but it was certainly true.

Colin had gone quiet again, staring into the flames as if they held a secret meant only for him. Kara wondered what he was thinking. For her, sitting around a campfire had always been a time to dream, make up stories, or watch the flames and think of nothing at all. She sighed and felt a sense of contentment as her body grew warmer and her muscles began to relax.

The sky had turned a dull gray, wrapping everything around them—trees, ground, and river—in a thick, damp mist. She felt too sleepy to move, as if she were bundled in a damp cotton quilt.

Colin stirred and added another small log to the fire. "How about those hot dogs? I'm so hungry I could eat an entire cow!"

Reluctantly, Kara pushed to her knees. She dug deep into her pockets and pulled out the package of wieners and a baggie that held mustard samples left over from meals at the Burger Barn. "The dried fruit and candy bars are in my saddlebag. I wish we'd brought coffee."

"Well now, little lady, you can't be expected to think of everything." Colin stood and swaggered over to where the horses were tethered just a few yards away. Kara rolled her eyes and turned her back to the fire. When Colin returned, he tossed something over her shoulder. It landed with a plop into her lap.

She scrambled back around. "Freeze-dried coffee—Colombian." She tried not to smile. "Well, looks like you are good for something after all."

She hoped he knew she was teasing. But he was busy arranging the aluminum coffeepot on a small, flat rock he'd already positioned at one edge of the fire and didn't take the bait.

81

Her fingers wouldn't cooperate as she struggled to open the vacuum-sealed package. She finally gave up and tossed it back to Colin. He caught it in midair, flipped open his pocketknife, and slit the top. The aroma made her mouth water, and her stomach growled in anticipation.

Colin grinned. "You sound like a half-starved bear cub."

Her stomach once again told her she was hungry. They both laughed. "More like the mama bear just out of hibernation. What time is it, anyway?"

He looked at his watch. "Almost one o'clock. Hard to believe we've been out here that long."

While the coffee perked, Wakara dipped her hands into the icy creek, dug up some sand, scrubbed, and rinsed.

"You've done this before." Colin knelt next to her, cleaning his own hands and the ends of two sticks he'd found on the ground.

She nodded. "Dad's been taking us camping ever since I can remember. I caught my first fish when I was three. Greg used to tease me when we were younger and say I should have been a boy, but Dad insisted we all learn camping and survival skills. Mom said Greg was jealous because it came so easy for me." She stood and waved her hands in the air to dry them. "Maybe it has something to do with my heritage."

"You mean your great-grandmother?"

Kara nodded. "I guess it makes sense; if I look the most like her, I must have inherited more of the Native American genes. I've always loved being outdoors."

Strands of hair from her braid had gotten caught in the zipper of her jacket. Colin reached down and began to work them free. "Hold still. I don't want to hurt you."

She froze in place, praying he wouldn't see the flush that had crept over her face. She wasn't nearly as afraid of having her hair pulled as she was of the way she felt when Colin

82

stood this close. He may be part of the family, but she definitely did not think of him as one of her brothers.

"There." He gave the braid a gentle tug and brushed it back over her shoulder. For a few seconds his brown eyes stared into hers, then he dropped his gaze and turned back toward the fire. "Let's eat. We've still got a lot to do."

She clenched her fists for a minute to stop her hands from shaking, then followed him.

11

THE ROUND, GLASS KNOB at the top of the coffeepot bubbled a dark, rich brown. Colin poured the steaming liquid into two tin cups, while Kara carefully threaded a wiener onto each of the sticks. She held hers over the fire until it was heated through, then quickly dipped it into the flames to blacken the outside.

Colin laughed and held up his stick. "Another thing we have in common."

They dipped the hot dogs in mustard and washed them down with gulps of warm coffee. The tin cups warmed their hands, while the food and drink warmed their bellies. Between the two of them, they finished the entire package of wieners.

Colin ate three fruit sticks and his candy bar, then wiped his hands on his jeans. "Ah, much better. For now." He looked at his watch. "We'd better get on with it if we want to get back in time for dinner."

She had to laugh. "Good thing this isn't a real survival situation. We just devoured two days' worth of rations."

She gathered the trash, wadded it into a ball, and stuck it in the plastic-lined pocket of her backpack. Colin rinsed both cups, then used his jacket cuff to pick up the coffeepot and set it just to the side of the steadily burning flames. "We might want more of this later. It's not getting any warmer out here."

Kara hugged herself and stamped her feet to get the blood flowing in her legs. It was cold and damp away from the fire. She pulled on her gloves and moved toward the travois. "We've already got the packing down and started a fire. I say we move on with the shelter."

"I'm with you. How big, and where do you want to put it?"

Kara looked around the clearing. "How about over there." She pointed to a cluster of three good-sized trees with strong, thick limbs and heavy boughs. "Those look like they'd hold together in a hurricane. They would block the wind."

She unzipped her pack and dug out a roll of fishing line. "We can't forget to tell them they can use shoelaces or strips of leather from saddlebags or ties, but I always carry this. You can use it for lots of things."

Colin helped her gather up the three stout poles she'd found and carry them into the half-circle of trees.

They arranged the poles tepee-style, with the longest stretching out behind in a simple A-frame. Wakara bound the tops together with fishing line and helped Colin push the bottom ends securely into the ground. Then they covered it with one of the space blankets. Kara threaded more line through a darning needle and secured the cover to the two front poles with a dozen stitches on each side. They found enough rocks to hold the edges of the blanket flush with the ground. Then Colin pulled out his hunting knife and cut several pine boughs to lay over the top of the shelter. By stacking them from the ground up and weaving them

85

together, they got by without having to use any more fishing line.

When they were done, Kara could feel herself sweating inside her jacket and shirt. She unzipped the jacket. "Whew. I need to shake this out and get dry."

Colin just nodded and did the same with his heavy parka. She was glad to see he was as out of breath as she was.

The damp air did little to dry the inside of the jackets. She couldn't take her shirt off, of course, and they hadn't brought a change of clothes along. She'd have to remember to do that for the actual demonstration. She'd promised Mr. Jaminson the afternoon's outing would be as real as possible.

"Ready to try it out?"

She took a deep breath. "I'm game if you are." She ducked through the opening, turned around, and sat down at the back. Colin had to get down on his hands and knees to enter, and once he was inside, neither of them could move without jostling the other.

Kara drew her knees up to her chest and wiggled back as far as she could go. "I guess this is more of a one-man shelter."

Colin was facing her, still on his hands and knees. "But it would be real cozy in a snowstorm."

His breath blew warm against her cheek, and Kara closed her eyes, wondering what it would be like to be trapped in a storm with Colin in a shelter as small as a doghouse. She leaned her chin on her knees. "Well, it sure would keep us warm."

Her eyes flew open. Had she said that out loud? Colin was grinning, but already backing out.

"We forgot pine boughs for the floor. My jeans are soaked."

She realized the seat of her pants was wet too as she crawled out into the cold air.

Colin handed over her jacket and gloves. "I think we'd better get back. I don't like the looks of that sky."

She looked up. Dark clouds had formed, hovering like demons right over their heads. The tops of the trees began to sway as an icy wind blew through the clearing.

Colin was already stowing away the rest of the gear. "Here." He handed her the tin cup with about two inches of steaming coffee in the bottom. "Drink up. It'll help until we're on the move."

She could only nod as she realized her teeth were already chattering.

Colin poured the last of the coffee on the fire, then refilled the pot from the creek and doused it again.

They stashed the unwashed cups in their backpacks, strapped them on, and untied the horses. Colin gave her a leg up, then mounted Dakota in one smooth stride.

"What about the travois?"

"We leave it."

"What about all that wood!"

"We leave that too." He turned and looked at her, his mouth set in a grim line, a look in his eyes that Kara had never seen before. A haunted look—something close to panic. He reached across the space between them and gripped her wrist.

"I don't mind practicing survival techniques, Wakara, or even teaching them, but we've both experienced the real thing, and I, for one, don't want to go there again. Ever."

She could only nod, remembering the fire, the heat, and the terror she felt when she knew both she and her little brother could die. They had been able to escape the heat and flames and spend the night in relative safety. It must have been far worse for Colin. Finding Anne injured and unconscious, racing on horseback up a trail he couldn't see, with a raging inferno burning on every side. When they fell and lost the horses, he'd had only enough strength left to drag Anne into a cave and wait for rescue. That must have been the longest and most agonizing two days of his life.

Kara urged Lily forward, and the mare was only too eager to go. The wind picked up, snapping like gunshots through the trees. When she looked over her shoulder, Colin was right behind her. Menacing dark clouds rolled after them, as if the storm was chasing them down the trail.

She gave Lily her head. Thanks to their earlier effort, the trail was clear of brush and debris, and the horses had traveled it dozens of times.

Lily might know the trail, but she hated wind. As the howling increased, so did the mare's speed, until Kara felt she was flying almost weightless, like in her dream, but this time it wasn't a happy feeling. The boiling clouds and screeching wind made her think of billowing smoke and the roar of flames that had chased her and her little brother down the nearly dry riverbed. She bent over the horse's neck, letting her run.

She saw the tree a split second after she heard the crash. A huge ponderosa pine hit the ground just a few yards in front of them. She bent lower, felt the horse's muscles bunch, the hind legs gather and push. Then they were going up and over, sailing through the air, front feet down, then the back. Kara rocked with the motion, and Lily never broke stride.

"Yee-haa!" Colin's yell split the air like the crack of a whip. Wakara didn't dare look, but she could still hear the thud of Dakota's hooves behind her. She could only pray Colin was still in the saddle.

They broke out of the clearing and into the meadow, where the clouds hovered and a cold rain had begun to fall.

Kara sat back in the saddle, loosened her grip on Lily's flanks, and tugged gently on the reins. The mare instantly obeyed by slowing her pace, then settled into a slow trot as they reached the field behind the barn. Kara drew her up beside the gate and dared to look behind her.

Colin's hat had disappeared, and his face was the color of dirty chalk. Dakota had slowed to a walk, and when they came up beside her, instead of the terror she expected to see, Colin was grinning from ear to ear.

"Whew, what a ride! For a few minutes I thought I'd signed up for a rodeo. Where did you learn to jump like that?"

Kara had the gate unlatched and shoved it open with her boot. "I didn't." She meant to explain that Lily had jumped while she just held on, but then the sky opened up and dropped a bucket of water on her head.

Colin latched the gate and they galloped to the barn. Instead of stopping outside to dismount, which was a basic rule, they rode the horses straight into their stalls.

Kara dismounted and had to grab hold of the saddle to steady herself. Her legs felt like jelly. Lily was blowing hard, her sides heaving, thick, white foam running from her mouth. Kara wrapped both arms around the horse's neck and gave her a long hug. The mare blew, then nuzzled her shoulder. "Good girl," Kara told her. She didn't have the breath to say more.

She moved quickly to pull the saddle and blanket off Lily's back. She could hear Colin mumbling to Dakota in the next stall. The big gelding was breathing every bit as hard as Lily. At one point, Kara thought she heard Colin moan.

She backed out of Lily's stall and peeked around the corner. Colin stood hunched over, one hand on his horse's bridle, the other clutching his ribs. The ride must have really jarred him.

"Colin?"

He tried to stand up straight, but then coughed and doubled over again.

Kara felt a jolt of fear. Had one of his ribs broken free and punctured a lung? After the fire, the doctor had told them Colin was lucky that very thing hadn't happened in his fall. Broken ribs would heal—and they'd been healing fine up to now—but a punctured lung was a different story.

She rushed into the stall and slid an arm around his back. The wheezing sounds coming from his chest scared her even more. "Can you walk?"

He nodded weakly, and she guided him through the barn and settled him on a bale of hay. While he caught his breath, she ran to the tack room and wetted down a handful of paper towels.

"Here," she spread one open and handed it to him. "Breathe through this, it will calm the cough."

He nodded and took it from her, placing it over his mouth and nose. The coughing slowed, and his breathing became more normal. Kara drew a deep breath of her own. "Whoa, you scared me." She picked up his wrist and found his pulse. It was galloping as fast as the horses had been a few minutes ago. But even as she started to count down one minute, Colin's heart rate slowed, and he rested his free hand on her arm.

"Wakara, it's okay." He used the paper towel to mop his face and neck, then wadded it up and accepted another to wipe his hands.

Wakara felt a tiny thrill at the way he said her name, but she wasn't sure she believed his words. "Are you sure you're okay? I think we'd better get you into Urgent Care and let a doctor look at those ribs."

Colin smiled and shook his head. "Thanks, but I'm really fine. The ride just set me back a little. The doc said I might have spells like this."

Still, she wasn't convinced. "I can drive the pickup, you know. I've got my permit, and with you in the car . . ." He was already shaking his head, so she let the sentence go unfinished.

Colin pushed to his feet. "We'd better get to these horses, or we'll be calling a vet."

"Right." She wanted to protest that she would rub down the horses and he should go to the house, but the set of his shoulders told her it would do no good.

On her way back to Lily, she peeked into the smaller stall at the far end of the barn.

"Colin?"

"Right here." He moved toward her slowly, lugging Dakota's saddle, still in obvious pain. But his breathing seemed to be okay.

She pulled herself up on the railing to get a better look inside the stall. Just as she thought, it was empty. "Did you turn Star out this morning? I thought we agreed it was too cold."

"We did." Colin peered over her shoulder. "Maybe Ryan let him out."

"He better not have," Kara fumed. "He knows better than to do something like that without supervision."

Colin shrugged. "Well, no one else is here. I can't see Anne tromping out here in that cast."

He was right. "I don't like this, Colin." Kara said. "I can't believe Ryan would take him out." She hopped down from the railing. "And listen to that storm!"

The pounding of rain on the barn's metal roof had turned staccato, fast and sharp as buckshot.

91

"Hail," Colin said, "or sleet. Sounds like it's coming down pretty good. I hope that pony isn't out in this."

"He has to be. He isn't here." She quickly scanned the barn. It was fairly small, with three stalls, a tack room, and two small sections for hay and sawdust storage. A wide center aisle allowed them room to groom and saddle the horses.

She turned and went into the tack room. Colin stowed his saddle, then joined her at the window. From that vantage point they could see a good portion of the south pasture where Star was usually allowed to graze. The cattle were huddled in and around a large stand of trees, which was shelter enough during a normal rainstorm. Kara wondered if it was really enough for this weather. "I don't see him."

"Neither do I, but he could be packed in there with the herd."

Colin flipped a switch, and she heard a buzz as the heat lamp turned on. "If the temperature drops much more, we'll have to move all those critters to the shed."

His shoulders drooped, and she knew he was as exhausted as she was—maybe more.

"We won't worry about that right now."

"Right. We'd better find that dad-blamed pony." He mopped his forehead with the sleeve of his jacket and reached for a lead rope. "Why don't you go on up to the house and ask Ryan. I'll wade into the fray and see if Star is with the cattle."

Kara felt torn. Lily and Dakota needed to be rubbed down and fed, but Star was older. If he was loose in this kind of weather it could be a matter of life and death.

She zipped her jacket and headed for the front of the barn. The sliding door scraped heavily along the grooves, and she opened it only enough to squeeze through. One look at the driveway and she froze.

"Oh, no!"

"What is it?" Colin poked his head through the door.

She felt like someone had punched her in the stomach, and she didn't know whether to pray or run. "Look." She pointed toward the house.

Sheriff Lassen's Land Rover was parked smack in the middle of the drive.

12

KARA LOWERED HER HEAD against the stinging sleet and sprinted for the house. She ran up the steps to the porch and nearly collided with Sheriff Lassen, who was just coming out the front door. "Hey there, little lady, slow down before you get hurt." He took hold of her shoulders to steady her, then stepped aside and ushered her into the house, holding the door for Colin, who was right behind her.

Anne was sitting on the sofa, wiping her eyes with a tissue and talking on the phone.

When Kara caught her breath, she spun around to face the sheriff. "What's wrong?" She felt a sinking sensation in her stomach. "It's Ryan, isn't it? Something's happened to him."

Sheriff Lassen pushed back his hat and wiped his brow with the back of his hand. "Now, Missy, don't get all heated up. The boy's probably holed up at a friend's house." He nodded in Anne's direction. "Miz Lightfoot is making some calls. Meantime, my deputy and I will have a look around—he hasn't been gone all that long."

Star! She grabbed the sheriff's arm. "Ryan's pony isn't in his stall. He must have taken him."

Colin had sunk down on the ottoman, holding his ribs. "Well, he didn't take the trail. We just came that way and didn't see any sign of him."

His voice sounded raspy, and Wakara knew he was really hurting. "Yeah, but we were riding pretty hard. We could have missed something."

Colin was shaking his head. "Not unless he's in the woods—trail's too narrow. The meadow and pasture were clear except for that bunch of cows."

Kara shuddered. If Ryan and Star had somehow gotten mixed up with the cattle, he could have been trampled.

Colin must have read her mind. "He could be up a tree, or under one." He stood and slapped his hat back on his head. "I'll go check it out."

But the sheriff stopped him. "Boy, you look like something a coyote spit out. You'd better take a breather." He glared at Wakara. "You too, Missy. Put on a pot of coffee, get yourselves warmed up, and let me do my job." He stepped outside and closed the door firmly behind him.

Wakara stiffened. She hated it when anyone called her Missy, not to mention the fact that the sheriff was treating her like a child. But there wasn't time to worry about it. Where could Ryan have gone?

She glanced out the window. The hail had stopped, but the lawn, pasture, and even the gravel drive had disappeared under a sheet of white ice. The sky still hung heavy and dark as lead.

The sheriff had reached his patrol car and started the engine. She watched him drive down to the barn and let his deputy out of the car. The younger man slid through the narrow gap they'd left in the sliding door and appeared a few seconds later, picking his way through sleet-coated mud

95

and a sea of hoofprints that pocked the pasture like craters on the moon. Kara knew it would be slow going. The tree stand where the cattle huddled was at least a hundred yards away.

Anne hung up the phone. "He is not at Campbells', or Smiths'." Her voice cracked. Kara turned from the window and joined her on the couch.

"What happened, Anne? How long has he been gone?"

Anne shook her head. "After lunch, he went to gather apples. One hour later, he is gone."

Kara frowned. "We know he took Star. He had to. That pony didn't get out by himself, but which direction did they go?"

"Not out the front," Anne said. "I would have heard them."

"And not on the back trail," Colin repeated his earlier thought. "Star would have been right in front of us, headed for the barn."

Colin was right. If Star had smelled the storm and heard the wind, he'd have hightailed it home, rider or no rider. If Ryan had fallen, he could be anywhere, hurt and unconscious . . . She shook away the thought. Star hadn't turned up either. The two of them must still be together. *Or both of them are hurt.*

She couldn't dwell on that.

"Who have you called?" she asked Anne.

"Everyone. They all search."

Wakara took hold of Anne's hand and squeezed it. "Then you've done all you can." Anne must feel so frustrated. Because of her cast she couldn't even canvas the yard, let alone the neighborhood.

"We have to think. He's never ridden alone before. Where would a six-year-old go?"

"You think. I will pray." Anne closed her eyes and raised her face to the ceiling.

Kara went back to the window. The deputy was no longer in sight, but cows were bellowing and scattering in all directions. The Land Rover was gone. Sheriff Lassen must have taken off on his own to search. The nearest neighbors were the Carlsons, and their ranch was a good five miles down the road. It would take hours, even days, to check out every ranch or homestead in the area.

He's not on the road. She frowned at the thought. *If he wasn't on the road or the trail through the woods, or in the pasture where he would normally ride, where else could he be?*

"The footpath!" She must have screamed it, because Colin jumped and Anne's eyes flew open.

"What footpath?" Colin limped toward her and took her place at the window. She was halfway to the door.

"Anne," she yelled back over her shoulder, "get Mr. Carlson on the phone. Tell him to send Dennis and Davie out to our path. They'll know what I mean." She let the door slam.

"Wakara, wait!" The screen door squeaked, and Colin grabbed her arm. "Where are you going?" He turned her to face him and softened his voice. "Look, let the sheriff search, okay? He knows what he's doing. They'll find him."

She pulled away. "They'll never look there."

He stepped in front of her. "Where? For Pete's sake, slow down and at least tell me where you're going."

She knew he was right. She needed to stop reacting and, as Dad would say, use her head. "There's another trail, just a footpath really, about a quarter mile long. When we were kids, the Carlson twins and I used it as a shortcut to each other's houses. If Ry took Star and rode out to the north side of the meadow, he could have mistaken it for a trail. It gets pretty narrow, but I think a pony could make it."

Colin frowned. "A quarter mile? That doesn't make sense—Ryan's been gone since lunchtime. He'd have made it to the Carlsons' by now."

"That's just it. Don't you see? If he did take that path, and the Carlsons haven't seen him, it means he didn't make it." Visions of her little brother trapped or lying injured from a fall quickened her sense of urgency. She spun around and jumped off the porch.

"Wakara!" Anne's voice stopped her. "Mr. Carlson has found Star."

The next half hour was a blur. Anne called the dispatcher to alert Sheriff Lassen and his men, while Colin grabbed the keys to Dad's Trooper and tossed them to Kara. "You drive. I'm too sore."

Kara drove as fast as she could under these conditions. When she finally reached the Carlsons', the car skidded to a stop, just missing the pole that held the boys' basketball hoop.

Mrs. Carlson met them in the yard. "That pony's in the barn filling his belly with oats. The Mister went after the twins." She pointed across a paddock to the small stand of woods that separated the two ranch properties.

"Oh, thank God, there they are! Looks like they found him," Mrs. Carlson suddenly exclaimed.

The four of them came from the tree line, Dennis toting his ever present rifle, Davie with Star's saddle slung across his shoulder, and Mr. Carlson carrying Ryan as he would a baby in a front pack. The boy's arms and legs were latched so tightly around the older man's neck and waist that Kara had to pry him off.

"Is he all right?"

"Think so." Mr. Carlson panted as he set Ryan down and bent over, hands on his knees, to catch his breath.

Ryan started to howl and buried his head in Kara's stomach. His clothes were wet clear through, and his hands felt like they were freezing. Before she had a chance to check him out, the sheriff's Land Rover pulled into the drive and squealed to a stop next to the Trooper.

"Doesn't look like he's hurt that bad," Mr. Carlson yelled over Ryan's screams. "The boys found him walkin' down the path, dragging the saddle and kicking pinecones." He chuckled. "Mad as a pestered hornet. Then he sees me comin' and puckers right up. Couldn't get a word out of him. Looks like cuts and bruises far as I can tell, but I'd get someone to check him over."

Kara wanted to shake her little brother for all the trouble he had caused. Instead, she knelt down and held him. He was probably scared to death. She might as well let him cry it out. Mrs. Carlson wrapped a blanket around both of them, and after a few minutes the screaming stopped, but he clung to her and refused to budge.

"Ry, are you hurt?" From the force of his grip she didn't think anything was broken, but she knew that sometimes fear caused an injured person to do things they shouldn't logically be able to do. She'd read about a man who had climbed all the way down a mountain after a fall and driven home with a broken back.

She felt his legs and arms as best she could. "Ry, I can't help you if you don't cooperate. Let go and let me look." She hated to be harsh with him if he was in pain, but they couldn't just sit here all day.

The sheriff knelt beside her and pressed his fingers to the pulse in Ryan's neck. "Hey, boy. You just relax now. We're gonna get you fixed up." He caught Kara's eye and winked. "Medics are on the way."

Ryan went still, then pushed back enough so they could see his face. "You called 911?" His eyes were wide beneath red and swollen lids. Kara found a small cut on his forehead and another on his chin. They had both quit bleeding a while ago.

The sheriff nodded soberly. "Sure. When someone falls off their horse, we check to see if they busted something. That's the rule."

Ryan stared at him. Kara couldn't tell if the look on his face was fear, pain, or anger. "I didn't fall. Stupid Star got spooked and ran me into a tree. I was hanging on good, but the saddle slipped and I had to bail out," he looked at her, "you know, like you told me before. Stupid Star runned away. I heard that ole cougar in the bushes, so I climbed a tree."

"Cougar?" The sheriff's eyes narrowed, and he stared intently into Ryan's face. "You sure about that, boy?"

Ryan just glared at him, so Wakara tried. "Did you see the cougar, Ry?"

Finally, he shook his head. "No. But it was there! The bushes kept rattling, and I heard it breathe—*Pouf*—like he was blowin' his nose."

Sheriff Lassen cleared his throat, and Kara's muscles relaxed. "That wasn't a cougar, Ry. It must have been a deer."

Someone laughed, and Kara realized Colin was standing right behind her. "Hey, Sport, are you telling me you spent all this time up a tree?"

Ryan scowled. "It's not funny. It could have been the cougar Dennis and Davie saw. Then it started raining hard, so I stayed there until it stopped, then I started walking 'til I found them." He pointed to the twins, who were sitting on the porch steps with their dad.

They heard one blast of a siren as the ambulance, lights flashing, pulled into the yard. Ryan's eyes grew wide. "Do I get to ride in that?"

"Sure do." The sheriff winked at Wakara again, stood up, and went to greet the paramedics.

"I don't think that's necessary," she called after him, but Colin lay a hand on her shoulder.

"He needs to be examined anyway. Might as well let him go with them."

Ryan started to cry again as the medics examined his head and neck, then strapped him to a stretcher. "The cut is small," one of them told Wakara, "but there's a good-sized bruise on his temple. Besides that, he's pretty cold and wet. I think we'd better take him in."

When they loaded him into the ambulance, Kara realized she was shaking. He could have a concussion, hypothermia, or something else they might have missed.

She started to follow Ryan to the ambulance, then remembered Anne. "Please wait a second," she called out to the medics, then turned to Colin. "We need to call Anne and let her know we found him."

"I already called." Mrs. Carlson slipped a warm paper bag into Colin's hands. "Chocolate chip cookies. If I know boys, he'll be hungry by the time they're done with him.

"And don't worry about the pony. We'll give him a bed for the night, and the boys can bring him home in the morning." She gestured toward Mr. Carlson and the twins, who were now standing by the patrol car talking with one of the deputies.

"Thanks, Mrs. Carlson, for everything." Kara gave the woman a hug, then hurried toward the ambulance. Colin was already in the car.

13

"HE'S DOING FINE, CONSIDERING," the doctor said. "None of the cuts need stitching, but he does have some bruises and a slight concussion." He studied the chart. "No frostbite or hypothermia. Good thing he got out of the tree and started walking when he did." He lowered the chart and looked seriously at both of them. "I want you to know, I chewed him out about not wearing a helmet. If you could see some of the riding accident cases we get in here . . ."

Kara nodded. "I know. It won't happen again." For some reason she felt guilty, as if she had been the one to let him ride without a helmet. But Ryan had always worn a helmet, even when he was little and she or Greg would lead him on one of the older horses up and down the drive.

". . . Watch him for a few more hours," the doctor was saying, "then you can let him sleep."

She nodded and slumped in the chair next to Colin. "If I had been there, he would never have taken Star without permission," she told him while they waited for the nurse to bring Ryan out.

Colin looked amused. "What makes you think that? He got past Anne, didn't he?"

"I guess. But Anne can't move very fast with that leg, and Ryan's a handful. I shouldn't have expected her to watch him alone."

Colin turned in his chair and studied her face. "You can't be serious!" He shook his head. "Wakara, none of this is your fault, and if you give Ryan even a hint that you think it is, you won't be doing him any favors. I was his age once, and I know."

He dropped his gaze, but she continued to stare at him. *Where is this coming from?* she wondered.

He must have sensed her confusion because he continued, "My mom felt so guilty about me not having a father that she let me get away with stuff most kids would have been punished for. And look where it got me." His eyes locked on hers again, and his voice sounded so urgent. "Mom handled her guilt by getting drunk. I handled my freedom by doing stuff that could have killed me or destroyed someone else's life. When I got caught, I always blamed it on someone or something else. If it weren't for that youth camp and finding Jesus, I'd be in prison by now, or maybe even dead."

She looked down at her lap as tears flooded her eyes. She got the point, but what was she supposed to do about it? "What should I do?" she asked out loud. "We can't reach Dad until Mark flies the radio in on Monday. I can ground Ry from riding Star, but I don't think he wants to ride anyway. He keeps trying to blame all of this on the pony."

Colin nodded as if to say, "See what I mean?"

She did see, and the more she thought about it, the more she felt like spanking Ryan. She wouldn't, of course, but Colin was right. Her little brother wasn't going to get away with this one.

An aide met them in the hall with Ryan, who was dressed in a pair of hospital pajamas, riding in a wheelchair. He clutched a plastic bag of wet clothes on his lap and refused to look at her.

Kara gritted her teeth. *Oh boy,* she thought, *you just wait until Dad gets home!* She and Greg had always laughed at that phrase, probably because their mom never used it. Dad's discipline was tough, but if he wasn't there, Mom usually took care of it right away.

Okay, Mom, so what should I do?

She rode in the back with Ryan on the way home, while Colin drove slowly through town. Streetlights lit up the wet blacktop as they drove. They stopped at two signals before turning onto the highway that led to the ranch. Traffic was light. Saturday night was no big deal here. The most Lariat had to offer was dancing at Rodeo City or bowling in a bowling league. Kara sighed. She would rather be throwing gutter balls at the bowling alley than dealing with this sullen, miserable little boy.

"Give it up, Ry," she told him when he started complaining again about all the things Star had done wrong. "No one is responsible for this mess but you."

He started to cry again, but she just handed him a tissue and went on. "You broke every riding rule there is, AND," she stopped him when he started to interrupt, "you scared everyone to death! Especially Anne. Why did you sneak away like that?"

He looked up at her, a puzzled expression on his tear-streaked face. "You know. If I'd told Anne, she would have said wait 'til you get back, and I didn't want to wait. Besides," his chin jutted out like it always did when he was being stubborn, "after Star runned away the first time, Colin said the best thing I could do was get back on the horse." He lowered his voice to mimic Colin, and Wakara almost laughed out loud.

Colin suddenly had a coughing fit, and she thought he was going to run the car off the road.

She tried to make her face look as stern as Mom's always had when Ryan pulled one of his stunts, but it was hard. "Not alone, Ryan. You know that. You never, ever ride alone until you are older and pass all the basic tests. I don't even ride alone very often."

"Colin does."

Kara sighed. "Colin is almost a man. Like it or not, you are still a little boy. And you'd better have something to say to Anne the minute we get home."

He frowned. "What?"

She wanted to shake him. "An apology, that's what. Then you go to your room and stay there until I can get ahold of Dad. Got it?"

"Dad?" Ryan's shoulders drooped, and the defiance went out of him like a popped balloon.

They pulled into the drive, and Colin stopped in front of the house. Anne had the front door open before they even climbed out of the car.

"He's fine," Kara called up to the porch.

Ryan broke away from Kara and ran into Anne's arms. "I'm sorry, Anne. I won't do it again, I promise," Kara heard him sob as she climbed the three front steps. She noticed Anne's color was better, and she looked more relaxed than when Kara and Colin had left her. *No wonder,* Kara thought, *she knows Ry is safe now.*

Ryan went to his room without complaint. Anne said little, but fixed him a tray with chicken noodle soup and a slice of corn bread from the night before.

"Thanks," Kara said. "I'll take it up. He said he wasn't hungry, but he needs to eat something."

"There is more in the kitchen," Anne said. "You and Colin must also eat." She turned away, and Kara noticed she was moving even slower than usual.

"Are you all right, Anne?"

105

"I am fine."

But Kara could tell by her tone that it wasn't true. Then it hit her. Anne must be feeling guilty, just as she had. But neither of them could have known Ryan would pull a stunt like that. The only way to stop him would have been to watch him constantly, and he was too old for that.

She would talk to Anne, she decided as she carried the tray up to Ryan's room. He was the one who had disobeyed, and what Colin had said about not allowing her guilty feelings to excuse Ryan applied to Anne just as well as it did to her.

14

RYAN'S COUGHING WOKE WAKARA at 6 A.M. She pushed back the covers, grabbed a pair of sweatpants and her flannel shirt, and went to check on him. Colin met her in the hall. He was barefoot, but had on jeans and a white T-shirt. His eyes were bloodshot, and his blond hair stood up at odd angles all over his head. Except for the stubble of beard on his cheeks and chin, he looked like a sleepy four-year-old as he stood there rubbing his eyes with his fists. She would have laughed, except she knew she looked just as bleary-eyed.

"Good morning." Colin yawned hugely and nodded toward the door. "He's been coughing like that for half an hour. I was just going down to wake Anne and see if there was something she could give him."

"Go ahead. I heard water running in the kitchen, so I think she's already up." Kara stifled a yawn. "There's cough syrup in the medicine chest downstairs."

Ryan coughed again, a deep, rattling sound. She tiptoed into the room. He was still asleep, lying on his side, legs drawn up and hands folded under his head on top of the pillow. When he coughed, his whole face screwed up in one

107

gigantic frown, then relaxed as he settled back into his dreams.

His skin looked flushed. The bruise on his temple had deepened to a purple-black blotch as big as a silver dollar, but the cuts on his chin and cheek were already scabbed over. She felt his forehead. *No need for a thermometer,* she thought; he obviously had a fever.

He moaned and rolled over just as Colin entered the room. "How is he?"

"I think he has bronchitis again. He's running a fever, but I don't think it's too high."

Colin stretched and ran a hand through his hair. "Anne's making one of her special teas. She wants me to bring him downstairs so she can treat him." He looked at her. "That okay with you?"

Kara nodded. "Sure."

"Good." Colin sat on the edge of the bed and began tugging on socks and boots. "She's already got a bed made up on the sofa in the family room."

Ryan moaned and opened his eyes when Colin picked him up to carry him downstairs. "My head hurts!"

"No doubt." Kara checked his pupils. They looked normal. She kissed his forehead. "Go on downstairs with Colin. Anne's got something to make you feel better, and I'll be down in a few minutes, okay?"

Instead of answering, he burrowed, snug as a sleepy kitten, against Colin's chest.

Wakara felt a rush of love for her little brother. He could be such a pain; sometimes she forgot he was only six.

She showered quickly and washed her hair. Sunday school didn't start until 9:30, so she could let it dry naturally instead of using the blower. She usually just braided it while it was still wet, but she wanted to wear it down today. As she combed conditioner through the thick, black locks, her conscience stirred uneasily. She really should offer to stay home with Ryan and give Anne a break. She felt a surge of disappointment; she really wanted to sit with Colin in church.

She peered into the mirror, expecting to see a little devil sitting on one shoulder and a tiny angel sitting on the other. "All right, you win!" she told the imaginary angel. "I'll offer to stay home. But if Anne says no, then you leave me alone. Deal?" She grinned at the silly charade, pulled on slacks and a bright red sweater just in case she did make it to church, then hurried downstairs.

Anne was in the kitchen. She shook her head when Kara repeated her offer. "No. I will stay."

Kara wrinkled her nose as Anne poured one of her special brews into Ryan's favorite mug. If this was the same concoction she had made a few weeks ago when Kara had a cold, it tasted as bitter as an unripe lemon. A teaspoon of honey would make it easier to swallow. She reached into the cupboard and handed Anne the honey jar.

Anne set it right back on the shelf. "Thank you, but sometimes a boy must take the medicine he earns."

Kara didn't dare laugh. Poor Ryan! It looked like there would be more consequences for his behavior than he'd counted on. And, she remembered, they still had to tell Dad.

Colin opened the back door just as Anne disappeared into the family room.

"Whew, who said July doesn't follow September? It must be 80 degrees out there."

Kara peered out the window at the thermometer. "More like 70, but you're right, you'd never know we had ice yesterday." She stepped outside, raised her face to the sun, and inhaled the balmy air. "Awesome! I'd better go find something cooler to wear."

Colin looked at his watch. "Eat first, we have plenty of time." He didn't look at her as he pulled a box of cold cereal off the shelf and grabbed a carton of milk from the fridge.

Kara gathered bowls, spoons, and the basket of fruit and set them on the table. By the time she poured juice and sat down, Colin was halfway through his first bowl of cereal. He finished off a banana, then cleared his throat.

"Uh, Wakara? If it's okay with you, I'd rather go into the college class today."

She stared at him, startled, then looked down at the table. It did hurt her feelings a little, but she hoped he wouldn't notice. "Sure," she managed, "they're more your age anyway."

That wasn't true, and they both knew it. Colin was only seventeen, but he'd been away from high school so long, she supposed he felt like he didn't fit in. She had guessed that the night of the football game. Or was it just that he wasn't interested in sitting with her anymore, and he was trying to let her down easy?

She took a sip of juice to try and swallow the lump in her throat, but Colin wasn't through.

"Nothing personal, okay? Mr. Andrews and I had a talk the night of the game. We decided it would be better if I went into the older group."

Kara looked up, but Colin was concentrating on filling his empty cereal bowl. Was that what he and Mr. Andrews were discussing when she got back to the bus the night of the game? And why was he so nervous about it? It wasn't like she had begged him to come to Sunday school, or to the game for that matter. She'd been so excited to have him along; maybe she had come on too strong.

She took a deep breath to gather courage. "Colin, have I . . ." She was about to ask if she'd said or done something to make him feel uncomfortable, but Anne chose that moment to come back into the room.

"We will have a hard winter, I think."

The Indian woman was standing at the window, but she might as well have sat down right between them.

"What makes you say that?" Colin asked.

"When Chinook Wind blows warm, Winter Warrior is not far behind."

"Excuse me," Wakara whispered. "I'm going up to change." She kept her napkin to blot her eyes and hurried up the stairs.

When she heard the car in the driveway, she came down and kissed Ryan good-bye. "Be good, mind Anne, and take your medicine," she warned him.

He made a face. "Yuck. She says I gotta drink that stuff two more times today."

Kara smiled. *Serves you right.* But she didn't say it out loud.

When Colin saw her coming, he climbed out of the driver's seat, opened the passenger door, and held out his hand to help her in. She looked at him, astonished, but he just grinned and drawled, "You look mighty pretty today, Miss Kara."

She wanted to sock him. One minute he acted like he didn't want to be with her, the next he was telling her she looked pretty—in that sick fake accent, of course. He couldn't be serious if his life depended on it.

She smiled brightly. "Why, thank you, sir," she mimicked his voice, "so kind of you to say so." She almost curtsied, but stopped herself in time. *Who's the fake, Wakara Sheridan? You chose this outfit on purpose.* She tried not to look smug. The short, white skirt looked fantastic against her sun-browned skin, and the turquoise blouse was the perfect accent for her long, black hair and sea green eyes. A narrow headband along with dangling turquoise-and-silver earrings completed the look. Yahi or Nez Perce? Whatever. She was proud of her heritage and wasn't afraid to show it.

111

She sat with Tia in church. Colin and some of the older boys sat in the row right behind. When the service was over, Kara hurried to the parking lot and climbed into the car without waiting for Colin to open the door. She just wanted to get changed, saddle Lily, and go for a nice, long ride. Alone.

When they pulled up to the house, it took her a minute to recognize the pickup parked in the drive. "Mark's here."

Colin nodded. "You go ahead and get out here; I'll park the car and be up in a few minutes."

She undid her seat belt and hurried into the house. Mark was at the kitchen table with Anne. He smiled and swallowed a bite of roast beef sandwich. "Hey, kid, looking good." He nodded at her outfit. "You just get in from a party?"

"Sure, I've been out all night."

"Not dressed like that you haven't." He winked at Anne. "Looks like I'd better drop off that radio and bring Harley on home."

She was used to his gentle teasing, and it was fun to tease him back. Mark was in his early thirties, single, but with lots of prospects. Besides being the best bush pilot in the county, he had been a friend of the family for years.

Wakara sat across the table from Mark, and Anne handed her a glass of iced tea. "Are you flying in today?" she asked him.

He nodded. "Sure. Thought I'd take advantage of this weather. From what I hear, it won't last long."

"Can I come?" It was out before she had a chance to think about it, but it would be a great time to see Dad, make sure he and Greg were okay, and tell him in person what had happened to Ry.

But Mark shook his head. "Sorry, kid, no room. I'm taking in hay. And that radio unit puts me right at the weight limit." He looked down at his empty plate. "Come to think of it, I probably shouldn't have eaten that sandwich." He

112

wadded up his napkin, carried his plate to the sink, and kissed Anne on the cheek. "Great meal, Sweetheart. If my plane goes down, I'll die a happy man."

Kara giggled in spite of her disappointment. Mark was the only one she knew who could make Anne blush.

On the way out the door, Mark squeezed Kara's shoulder. "You should hear from your dad tonight. I'll tell him to call you about seven o'clock. Other than that, my lips are zipped." He made a slashing motion across his mouth with two fingers.

"Seven's fine," Kara smiled in gratitude. He understood that she wanted to be the one to tell Dad about the incident with Ryan. She wanted Dad to get it straight the first time around.

Kara changed into shorts and a tank top. Instead of riding Lily, she decided to lie in the sun and read. She fell asleep about four o'clock, and before she knew it, Anne was calling her in for dinner.

Her skin felt warm, but the sun sinking behind the mountains left a chill in the air that reminded her more of yesterday's weather. She put her book away and went in to check on Ryan.

He was sitting up working a puzzle at a TV tray. "Hi, Ry, how are you feeling?"

He shrugged. "My head still hurts."

She felt his forehead. He was still warm, but his eyes were clear. "The doctor said it probably will for a while." She watched him move the puzzle pieces around hit-and-miss, and could tell he wasn't really concentrating. "Are you hungry? Anne has chili and beans for dinner."

"I'm not hungry." He finally fit a piece into the puzzle. "Wakara?" His voice was so soft she had to bend down to hear him.

"What?"

"When is Dad gonna call?"

113

So that was it. He was worried about talking to Dad. She couldn't blame him. She had seldom been in trouble as a child, but once or twice was enough to remember the fear of waiting to find out what her punishment would be. Dad was fair but strict, and disobedience was something he didn't tolerate.

"He's calling at seven o'clock. I'll talk to him first, then you can talk, okay?"

His mouth quivered. "I think I'll prob'ly be asleep by then."

She tried not to laugh. "I doubt it. You've been asleep most of the day." She decided to change the subject. "You're not coughing as much. It looks like Anne's medicine is working."

When he didn't answer, she pulled the TV tray away. "Dinner's ready, Ryan." She took his hand. "Come on, let me help you to the table. It's too hard for Anne to bring you a tray."

His face clouded in a scowl, but he didn't resist when she put her arm around his skinny shoulders and led him into the kitchen. Not that it did much good. He ate about two bites of chili, then asked to be excused.

Anne covered his bowl and put it in the refrigerator. "He will be hungry later."

15

DAD'S CALL CAME IN at seven o'clock on the dot.

"Good news, Sugar Bear! We cleared the trail down from Pinewood Meadow. It's pretty black over in there, but the trail is in good shape."

She felt relieved. Besides a bush plane, that trail was the only way into the valley and was popular with many of their guests. "What about Eagle Lodge?" she asked. "Did you get any work done there? Over."

"We managed to get that old barn boarded up. We're finishing off the roof on cabin three today. If we have time, we'll get a new corral built before the first snowfall."

With all the work left to do, when were they taking off on their scouting trip? She decided not to bring it up. They were already getting some static, and she still had to tell him about Ryan.

She kept the story brief, relating what he needed to know and checking from time to time to see if he was still with her. Other than acknowledging that he was still on the radio, he didn't interrupt. When she told him how she had handled the situation, he said, "You did fine, Wakara. Put Ryan on, then I'll talk to you again. Over."

Ryan approached the radio as if it were an electric chair. Kara almost felt sorry for him, but she stepped away and tried not to eavesdrop as Dad talked to him. Ryan nodded a couple of times and shook his head, but only spoke once to say, "I'm sorry, Daddy," then he handed the microphone to Kara. His eyes were full, but he didn't cry, and she knew Dad had been kind.

"Dad?"

"Okay, Sugar Bear, here's the scoop. We'll be home in five days. Until then, Ryan goes nowhere except to school. No Timmy's house, no horses. He's to help you clean the barn every day. He's old enough to work. Don't let him slack off."

She nearly groaned out loud. Help her clean the barn! Why did that make her feel like she was being punished too?

"Got it, Dad. When are you going . . ." She was interrupted by a whistling sound, like wind rushing through the trees.

"Wakara, are you still there?"

"Yes, but I think the signal's getting weak. Over."

"Okay. We're going to take advantage of this . . ." Static crackled in her ears, and she knew they were losing contact. ". . . Don't expect to hear . . ."

"Dad?" She twisted the frequency knob, but the line went completely dead, and she knew she'd lost him. What were they going to take advantage of? Probably the weather. Maybe they would get the corral done tonight or tomorrow. That would mean less work when they went back in June.

Ryan seemed to take his punishment in stride. He thanked Anne for reheating his dinner, gobbled down two bowls of chili, and even swallowed his last dose of medicine without complaint. His cough was much better, and his breathing seemed almost normal. Colin carried him back up to his room, and he was sound asleep by eight o'clock.

Kara didn't stay up either. She and Colin had planned to go over their strategy for tomorrow's demonstration, but she suddenly felt as if she'd been trampled by a herd of cattle. Colin was yawning too as they said goodnight. She crawled into bed and was asleep as soon as her head hit the pillow.

When she opened her eyes, the room was black as midnight. And so quiet. For a minute she wasn't sure she was really awake. A few seconds later a shrill beep caused her to prop herself up on her elbows. Then silence again, like the time they had toured the Oregon Caves. The guide had told them to turn off their flashlights and stand very still. The thick, black silence was both awesome and frightening, and she had been glad when they had turned the lights back on and resumed the tour.

She sat up in bed and shivered. It took another minute for her to identify the beeping sound that had awakened her. *Smoke alarm. Low battery warning.* She rubbed her eyes and glanced at the clock. The digital face was blank. *No electricity.* No wonder she was so cold. She groped for her sweat suit and slippers, then got the flashlight out of the drawer in her bedside table. She lifted the shade to her window and gasped. Snow! Coming down in sheets. *A whiteout.* Her flashlight could barely penetrate the gloom. She trained it where the apple tree should stand, then on the driveway and the pasture fence, but it was as if the world outside had become invisible.

The silence was broken by another shrill beep. Then she heard footsteps moving down the hall and a soft tap on her door.

"Kara? You awake?"

It was Colin. She shone the flashlight in front of her and went to the door.

"I'm up," she whispered, not wanting to awaken Ryan or Anne. "Do you know what time it is?"

117

He shined his own light on his watch. "It's 4 A.M. I'm worried about the cattle. They could freeze to death in a storm like this."

She groaned. On Saturday they had talked about gathering all the cattle into the winter sheds, but they had spent the day hunting for Ryan, and Sunday had been so warm, they had let it go.

"How could we know?"

Colin matched his voice to hers, and she could imagine him shaking his head. "Anne knew. Remember her comment about Chinook winds and Winter Warrior? I didn't pay much attention at the time. Now I wish I had."

Kara stared past Colin as they heard a rustling sound downstairs, then a soft whoosh as kindling caught in the woodstove. "Speaking of Anne . . ."

The glow of lantern light illuminated the figure at the bottom of the stairs. "Bring Ryan down, please. He must stay warm."

"On my way," Colin said, and Wakara watched his flashlight beam trail off down the hallway. When he reappeared cradling Ryan, who was wrapped head to toe in one of their mother's quilts, she focused her flashlight beam ahead of them on the stairs.

A few minutes later, Ryan was bedded down in the family room, undisturbed by the move. "He must really be zonked," she said to Colin as they shut the door and joined Anne in the kitchen.

She had started a fire in the wood-burning cookstove. It was an antique Mom had found at a store in Lariat, a little smoky, but it worked well in an emergency. An oil lamp burned in the center of the table, and the room had taken on a warm, cheery glow. While Anne measured coffee into the aluminum pot and set it on the woodstove to perk, Kara retrieved the battery-operated radio from a shelf on the service porch. Dad had talked about getting a NOAA Weather Radio receiver to monitor severe weather warnings, but when the equipment at the lodge had to be repaired, he had decided the NOAA radio would have to wait.

She turned on the small portable radio, keeping the volume low. Dad had made it clear that it was for emergencies only, and they kept it tuned to the all-weather station.

"The National Weather Service has issued a winter storm warning for all of eastern Oregon, with temperatures dropping into the low teens and below-zero conditions in the mountains. Motorists have been warned that driving conditions are extremely hazardous. State Police are investigating several stranded cars, and all roads have been closed to anything other than emergency vehicles." The newscaster broke in on a personal note. *"Stay home, folks. It's really nasty out there."*

Kara looked out the window. The sky had lightened to a hazy gray as millions of snowflakes blotted out the sunrise and piled, white on white, blanketing the ground.

"I hope Dad and Greg are okay." She couldn't help but worry. They would have to take care of the horses, and it was a long way from the barn to the lodge. Just a few weeks ago she'd read about a man who had gotten turned around in a blizzard and froze to death just a few yards from his cabin door.

Colin interrupted her thoughts. "They're fine. I'm sure they're snowed in, but we left enough dry wood in the shed to last the winter."

"And there is food," Anne added. "We closed early."

She was right. There had been lots of canned provisions, as well as some dried soup and beef jerky.

Then she remembered they had another problem. "What do we do about the cattle?"

Colin ran one hand through his hair, then rubbed his shoulder. He had told her once before that the cold made it ache. She could imagine how painful it must be today.

119

"We go get them as soon as it's full light. In the meantime we pray none of them have frozen to death."

"The wind blows light for now. They are cold, but in no danger." Anne poured coffee, set the aluminum pot aside, and replaced it with a pot of water.

"All the animals will need extra hay." Kara stretched and yawned. She used to like waking up to heavy snow. It meant a day off school, sledding or riding a toboggan down the hill at the top of their property. Today, she knew, would be different. "I'd say we've got our work cut out for us."

Instant oatmeal and toasted bread spread with Anne's homemade apple butter quieted the growl in Kara's stomach. When Colin stood, so did she.

"Wear lots of layers. We'll be working both outside and in the barns."

She bit back a sharp reply. Did he think she was stupid? She'd lived out here and tended stock a lot longer than he had. But as she climbed the stairs to her room, she relented. Colin had been living with an uncle in Alaska. He'd probably seen a lot more snowstorms in the past two years than she'd seen in a lifetime.

Most of the cattle were huddled by the gate, waiting to be let into the run-in shelter. It was really just a long, wooden, three-sided shed, but it faced away from the wind so the animals would be comfortable even in this weather. The cattle didn't need much prodding. Once Colin opened the gate from the lower pasture, the lead steer plunged through and the others followed. Kara and Colin shooed them past the barn, where Lily and Dakota were waiting, past the nearly renovated bunkhouse and into the shelter where they were soon munching contentedly on sweet green hay. The heifers and their calves were already snug in two enclosed stalls at one end of the shed, and the five working horses, which usually had free range in the upper pasture and woods, huddled by the feeders at the other end.

In just under three hours, they had fed and watered all of the animals and cleaned the stalls in the horse barn where Lily and Dakota practically inhaled their extra ration of grain.

Kara shivered as she and Colin stepped out of the barn. There had been a break in the weather about halfway through their chores, but now the sky had darkened again, and a new flurry of snow began to fall, pushed by a stronger, colder wind.

"Whoa!" Colin shouted as they tromped toward the house. "It's a good thing we're done. I think we're in for it this time."

The radio proved him right. Winter storm warnings had changed to blizzard warnings, which could be a disaster for any person or animal caught outside.

Oh God, Wakara prayed off and on throughout the day, *please keep Dad and Greg safe.*

They slept downstairs that night, rolled in sleeping bags in front of the fire. Everyone but Ryan took turns getting up to keep the woodstove blazing, and by morning Kara was sweating inside her bag. There was just enough light in the room to make out Anne asleep in the recliner, Ryan curled up on the sofa, and Colin snoring softly on the other side of the woodstove.

Kara crawled to the window, blinked, then stared at the steadily falling snow. Snow piled to the windowsill. Snow obliterating the sky and covering every square inch of ground.

She shook Colin awake.

"What? Wakara—what's wrong?"

"Shh." She put one finger to her lips. "Get up and come look. I think we're really trapped this time."

The room was warm enough, but she still had goose bumps as she followed him to the window. "We aren't going

121

to get to the barn anytime soon. And if it's this bad here, Dad and Greg are snowed in for sure."

"Holy smoke." Colin rubbed a spot on the glass and peered through the window. He shook his head. "You're right. I can't even see the barn. We'd better pray this lets up soon."

She tried to be practical. "We gave the animals double hay last night. They should be okay for a while."

Colin massaged the back of his neck and arched his shoulders, his forehead wrinkling in pain as he stretched. "Ahhh," he groaned and peered out the window in the direction of the barn. "I'm not in any real hurry to go out in that." He pointed to the window. "We'll give it a couple of hours, then figure out something."

Anne stirred, then sat up, and Colin helped her to her feet. She glanced out the window, but made no comment on the weather. "I will start the coffee," she said as she hobbled toward the kitchen.

Kara looked at her watch. "It's almost 7 A.M. I'm going to call Dad."

At 8:10, she finally gave up and clicked the off button on the transmitter.

16

WAKARA AND COLIN STEPPED outside just before noon. The blizzard had stopped, leaving behind it a world of white silence. A cold sun peeked from behind the mountains, and only a few of the more courageous birds had left their nests. They laughed as they watched a blue jay circle a snow-covered stump as if deciding how best to uncover a dinner of frozen bugs. A robin gave out a tentative *thwirrp* as it hopped from one foot to another on a tree branch, dislodging a load of snow, then it ruffled its feathers and settled down with another chirp of triumph.

The screen door slammed, and Anne came up behind them with a dish of bread crumbs. "The birds will go hungry if we do not help," she said, and handed the plate to Kara.

"Thanks, Anne. I'll scatter these here. We can use grain out by the barn."

"I'll get some birdseed next time I'm in town." Colin stepped down off the porch, and the powdery snow covered his boot tops.

"It's not too hard to walk in. Must not have gotten as cold as they expected."

Kara held on to the railing and stepped in Colin's footprints. The surrounding snow came almost to her knees. "Whoa. Maybe it's not hard for you to walk, but this is one of those times when I wish I could grow another six inches."

Colin turned and flashed her a grin. "Hang on to my belt. The snow isn't really packed. I think I can shuffle through and clear a path."

It was slow going, but Colin was able to clear a passable trail. By the time they reached the barn, she could tell he was tired and sore.

The butane heat lamps had burned out, and the animals were cold, but none of them seemed bothered by it. Star was still at the Carlsons'. They had a generator, and Kara knew he was warm, dry, and probably very content.

Lily nickered, and Dakota thumped the wall with his back foot, impatient for breakfast.

"Sorry, guys." Kara rubbed the mare's nose and checked her over. When she found no sign of frostbite or any other problems, she gave Lily grain, water, and enough hay to last two days, just in case the weather turned bad again. Then she and Colin went to tend the other animals. By the time they finished feeding and watering all the stock, Kara's hands and feet felt numb, even through fur-lined boots and gloves.

"Whew," Colin lifted his hat and wiped sweat from his brow. "That's work."

"Yeah," she agreed and joined him at the barn door. "Especially since there's only two of us."

She didn't add, "I wish Dad and Greg were here," but Colin must have known that's what she was thinking, because he slipped one arm around her shoulders and squeezed. "Your dad and Greg will be home soon, then we'll get even."

"Right." She smiled up at him, but couldn't stop the knot of pressure building in her chest. She had this nagging feeling that something was wrong, and nothing seemed to shake it. Not even prayer.

Colin gave her another squeeze, then stepped out of the barn, leading the way back along the same path.

"Oh. Wait." She stopped and called to Colin, who was a few paces in front of her. "All the equipment and supplies for the survival demonstration are still in the barn. Shouldn't we get them put away?"

Colin turned around. "Right now that barn looks like it's a hundred miles in the wrong direction. Besides, I'm sure the demonstration isn't canceled, just postponed. They'll probably reschedule for next Monday."

She nodded. "I hope so."

Back at the house Anne greeted them with hot soup and pan-fried corn bread.

"The phone still doesn't work," Ryan grumbled. "The TV neither, so I can't even watch John Wayne."

Kara felt sorry for him. She'd be restless too, cooped up all day with nothing to do. It was too bad he couldn't go out and play in the snow, but with him just getting over bronchitis, outside wasn't an option.

He looked so forlorn, Colin gave in and offered to play Chinese checkers.

A few minutes later, Kara excused herself from the table and went to try the radio again. After ten minutes she gave up and was about to leave the room, when the radio crackled to life.

"Wakara! Are you there? Like, can you believe this? They're saying there's another storm behind this one, and we're never going to get the electricity back. I can't use the computer at all, and my report is due next Tuesday! Wakara?"

Kara rolled her eyes. "Let go of the button, Tia," she said out loud, "then I can talk to you."

"What? I didn't get what you said!"

She tried again. "Hang in there, Tia. Let's try again. Over."

"Did you read me the first time? Over."

"Yes. I'm sorry about the electricity, but there's nothing we can do about it. It will take them days to get this cleared up. Over."

Tia moaned. "Days? I can't go days without a phone line. Like, what about all my e-mail?"

"Well, if it's any consolation, they'll probably get to you before they get to the lines out here."

"Yeah. You're right." Tia paused, and Kara could hear her talking to someone in the background. Then she said, "Pops wants to know if your dad made it home."

Wakara's stomach suddenly felt queasy. "No. And the radio's out up there. I can't get through at all."

"I hope they're okay. I mean, like, not trapped in an avalanche or something. If I were you, I'd get the Search-and-Rescue to check it out." There was more talking in the background, then Tia sighed. "Okay, okay. Wakara? Pops says I gotta get off in case there's an emergency or some-thing. I hope they're wrong about that other storm. I'll talk to you soon. Bye."

The receiver went dead, and Kara had to fight back tears. An avalanche! She couldn't believe some of the things Tia came up with. But what if it were true? The mountainsides had just been ravished by fire. The slopes could be really unstable. Anything could happen.

In the family room, she found Ryan curled up like a kit-ten with his head on Colin's lap and Colin sitting with his head thrown back against the sofa cushions, both of them fast asleep. For a moment, she studied Colin's face. With long, blond lashes that curled upward, a smooth, unlined forehead, and cheeks flushed from the heat of the wood-stove, he looked like a little boy. She quickly turned away. No way did she want Colin to wake up and find her staring at him.

Anne sat at the kitchen table reading a magazine and sipping a cup of tea. She looked up as Wakara walked through the door. "The boys are asleep?"

Kara nodded. "Yeah. I wish I could fall asleep that easily."

Anne's stare made her nervous. "You worked hard today. Sometimes the mind will not let the body sleep."

The woman was right on, as always.

"I just can't stop thinking about Dad and Greg," Kara admitted. "I just know something's wrong."

Instead of trying to encourage her as she normally would, Anne looked down as if studying the contents of her teacup. "If there is trouble," she finally said, "God knows about it."

Wakara's hands shook as she poured a cup of tea and carried it carefully to the table. She felt like she was going to burst into tears any minute. "Sure, but there's supposed to be another storm. If they don't get out now, they might be stuck there for the winter."

"If God is able to guide children through fire, can He not lead men through snow?"

Anne's gentle reminder should have made her feel better. Instead, she felt a flicker of doubt. She sipped the hot liquid, hoping it would ease the lump in her throat. "I know God's watching over them, but . . ." She stopped, trying to find the right words for what she was thinking. Anne didn't interrupt, just sat quietly watching, her eyes full of understanding.

127

Kara took a deep breath. "It's like God sees and He's with us and everything, but sometimes He lets bad things happen anyway." She sniffed back a tear, and Anne handed her a napkin.

"Thanks." She dabbed her eyes and blew her nose, but once they started, the tears wouldn't stop. Neither would the words. "I mean, Mom loved God. She prayed all the time. Every morning when I was leaving for school, she'd be sitting in the family room with her Bible and notebook, doing some kind of study.

"She used to tell me that God is our Father and loves His children more that any human parent ever could. I liked that." She tried to smile, but could feel her lips tremble and was afraid she would burst into tears again. Anne smiled gently in agreement, and Kara rushed on. "I believed it too. Thinking of God as my Father made me feel safe. Until the accident."

Her mouth felt like cotton, and she took another swallow of tea. "It's just that sometimes I wonder, if God loved Mom so much, why did He let her die?"

Her heart was pounding so hard it felt like it could leap out of her chest. It was like someone else was saying the words she had buried deep inside and wouldn't stop until she was empty—like an hourglass turned upside down.

"I'm God's child. So is Dad. And so is Greg; he became a Christian before I did. But God still took Mom away from us." She saw the tears running in rivulets down Anne's cheeks, but she couldn't stop.

"Ryan was only five years old! If God is so loving, how can He kill a little boy's mother?" She had to bite her lip to keep from shouting, and she didn't dare pick up her teacup or she would throw it at the wall.

"I can't trust Him anymore, Anne. Mom died. How can I be sure nothing will happen to Dad and Greg?"

Anne didn't bother to wipe her own tears away, but looked deeply into Wakara's blurry eyes. "You can't."

She said it so softly, Kara wasn't sure of what she'd heard. "What?"

"'In this world, you will have trouble, but fear not, I have overcome the world.' Jesus said that, Wakara. Do you understand?"

Kara shook her head. "No. I've heard that verse before, but I never really got it."

Anne closed her eyes, and when she spoke again, Kara wasn't sure if she was praying or talking to her.

"If a man walks on glass he will bleed. If I touch fire, I will get burned. If a lion does not kill, it suffers hunger, and a camel tethered by a dry well will die. Such are the troubles of the world."

"Well, yeah," Kara frowned. "But no one does those things on purpose, and most of us don't go around worrying about it."

Anne nodded. "Accidents happen. A lion grows too old to kill. Drought steals the water of life. Why then do we not live in constant fear?"

She didn't even have to think about that one. "Because we know it happens, but we hope it won't happen to us."

Even as she said it, she began to understand where Anne was going with this. Her heart rate slowed, and everything inside her went still. "Hope," she whispered, then looked up into Anne's gentle smile. "That's the key word, isn't it?"

"Where do you place your hope, Wakara?"

"In Jesus. At least that's where I'm supposed to."

"Why?"

"Because when Jesus died and rose again, He gave me a chance to live with God forever when I die." She wiped her eyes and felt a rush of understanding. "When Jesus said, 'I have overcome the world,' He meant He had overcome trouble and death on earth by giving us a way to live forever in heaven. Like Mom."

Anne leaned over, took Wakara's face between her hands, and gently kissed her brow.

17

THE SECOND STORM MOVED IN at 10 P.M. Even Anne admitted the men might be in danger. She and Colin agreed that Wakara should give up trying to reach Dad on the radio and contact Sheriff Lassen instead.

The sheriff sounded tired but sympathetic. "I'm sorry, Missy, but there's no way I can get Search-and-Rescue in there under these conditions. Visibility is a big fat zero, and it doesn't look like it's gonna let up anytime soon."

He went on about cars stranded on the Interstate and broken-down snowplows, then tried to reassure her. "Those radios aren't all that reliable. Your daddy's is probably on the blink." He chuckled. "Harley's got food, shelter, and the biggest fireplace in the state. You can bet those loafers are holed up in the lodge, drinking coffee and robbing each other blind with a deck of cards."

"He's right, you know," Colin agreed. "They're probably fine."

When Kara glared at him, he took her by the shoulders. "Look, this storm can't last forever. If we don't hear from them by the weekend, I'll saddle Dakota and ride in there myself, okay?"

The weekend! Kara fumed. Colin was as bad as the sheriff; they both treated her as if she didn't have a brain.

She twisted away from Colin's grip and headed for the stairs. "I'm going to bed. When the storm clears, I'm going to Eagle Lodge, with or without help."

Anne laid a hand on her shoulder. "Try to sleep, Wakara. And remember, daylight is wiser than dark."

In other words, don't make any rash decisions tonight. She was getting better at deciphering Anne's little sayings. She forced a smile. "Thanks, Anne, for everything." She knew the woman would understand that she meant their talk in the kitchen as well as her wise advice.

Her room was freezing! She left the door open a crack and turned on the butane heater. She took off her slippers, but left on her wool socks and thermal underwear, then crawled into bed and pulled the covers up over her chin.

"Take care of them, Lord," she whispered into the darkness. Still, she couldn't quite extinguish the flicker of fear that leapt in her stomach when she thought about Dad and Greg trapped in those isolated mountains. Even if they were in the lodge, they could run out of food or firewood, and what about the horses? The men had taken hay and grain, but would it be enough? She tossed and turned, trying desperately to make her mind blank so she could go to sleep. Finally, she resorted to a trick she had used as a child and began reciting silly nursery rhymes in her head.

It must have worked. When she awoke, her glow-in-the-dark watch read 2 A.M. She could make out the shape of her dresser, the computer desk, even the pile of books stacked on the floor in the far corner of the room.

Moonlight on snow! She felt a stab of pure joy when she realized the reason for the light.

She sat up in bed, turned around, and looked out the window. It had been so dark in the room when she had gone to bed that she had forgotten to pull down the shade.

A full moon floated in the coal black sky, reflecting a cold, white light off the blanket of snow. The wind had stopped, but tree limbs bowed low to the ground. She heard a loud crack as a tree branch snapped and landed with a soft plop, sinking deep into the soft, white powder.

"Awesome!" she whispered, then felt a sharp kick of fear. The feeling built until she turned around and jumped out of bed.

Something's wrong, isn't it, God? Dad and Greg need help. I know it!

A hundred thoughts crowded her brain. It had stopped snowing, but the tree branch had sunk, so the ground wasn't frozen solid. The full moon gave off plenty of light. Their supplies for the survival training class were still in the barn. Lily had traveled in snow before—all the horses had. Maybe she could get through.

"Not maybe!" she whispered, clenching her fists in determination. "I *will* get through." *Hold on Dad, I'm coming.*

She took off her sweatshirt, put on a long-sleeved T-shirt and black leggings over her thermal underwear, and then pulled the sweatshirt back over her head. Thank God her ski pants still fit.

I never ride alone. You scared everyone to death. You broke every rule! Why did you sneak away? The angel was on her shoulder again, reminding her of every word she'd said to Ryan.

Because if I had told Anne, she would have said to wait.

But this couldn't wait! Dad and Greg needed help, and in this kind of weather, every minute counted.

Her boots fit snugly over two pairs of socks. She grabbed an extra set of long underwear and two more pairs of socks, then scribbled a note for Anne.

Adrenaline spurred her on as she crept down the stairs. She peeked into the family room and counted heads. The drapes were drawn so the room was darker, but she could make out the forms: Anne in the recliner, Ryan curled up on the couch, Colin snoring softly from his sleeping bag closest to the woodstove. She ignored a stab of guilt. They would be worried about her, but that was good! Maybe then Sheriff Lassen would cooperate and send in the troops.

Her heavy parka and fur-lined gloves were in the mudroom. Thanks to the woodstove that Anne kept burning in the kitchen, they were warm and dry. She tugged them on, added a wool cap underneath the hood of her jacket, and eased open the back door. Careful not to let the screen slam behind her, she stepped out into the bright, clear night.

The first breath of crisp air made her gasp. *Whoa! Who said it wasn't cold!* Steam poured from her nostrils as she exhaled, and her eyes watered as she gazed into the still, white light.

"Okay, God," she whispered, "I know You're there. Keep me safe and help me find them, please?" She took a deep breath to calm her nerves. Blowing into her cupped hands, she drew the warm air back into her lungs, then straightened her shoulders and stepped off the porch into the snow.

The stuff underneath was packed, but the powdery surface would make it fairly easy to plow through. Five steps though, and she wished Colin were in front of her breaking trail. She turned and looked back toward the house. It looked solid and warm. She almost turned around. Should she wake Colin and somehow convince him to go with her? But what if he refused? Worse, what if Anne woke up? They would make her stay. She had to do this on her own.

It took nearly fifteen minutes to shuffle to the barn. Her feet were already numb, and she almost whimpered with gratitude as she stepped through the crack in the sliding door and inhaled warmer air.

The horses shifted in their stalls, and Lily blew softly in greeting. Kara reached through the bars and rubbed the mare's nose. "Hey, girl," she whispered, "you want to go for a ride?"

She gave both of the horses a half pad of hay to keep them quiet, then moved into the tack room. Quickly she sorted through the gear, stuffing what she needed into one set of saddlebags and one backpack.

She had grabbed a package of homemade trail mix from the kitchen; peanuts, raisins, dried fruit, and chocolate candy could sustain a person for days. Along with the fruit rolls, coffee, and elk jerky that they had left in the packs, she should have enough food.

Breathing a prayer of thanks that the men had insulated the pipes in the barn while they were doing the bunkhouse, she filled the two largest canteens and set them near the hay bales with the rest of the gear. She went back into the tack room to get Lily's saddle, but something was nagging at the edge of her consciousness. Something Anne had said to Colin after the fire.

The memory came as clearly as if they were standing in the room. "Lily was afraid," the cook had said when they visited her at the hospital. "Dakota is the horse to have when trouble comes." Wakara had felt a little insulted, but the mare *had* spooked and thrown Anne into a tree.

Kara thought about it. Dakota was bigger and stronger. His legs were long and solid, and his feet were huge—big enough to plow through snow. Up in Alaska, Colin had ridden the buckskin through worse weather than this.

Okay, Anne's right, she reasoned. *Dakota is the horse for this job.*

135

That decision made, she didn't waste any more time. It was thirty miles by road to the Pine Creek trailhead. Eagle Lodge nestled in the valley, another eight miles down the steep, switchback trail, and three more across open meadows. They had always driven the horses in a trailer from here to Pinewood Meadow, but that was impossible now. She would have to ride all the way.

She brushed Dakota, laid two cotton blankets and a pad across his back, then quickly lengthened the girth on her saddle. It was a little small for the big gelding. She thought about riding bareback, but quickly dismissed the idea. If the going got rough, she might need something to hold on to.

She led Dakota to the mounting block, stepped into the saddle, then hesitated. Which way? The road was out of the question. Someone might see her and make her turn back. The forest trail ended several miles from town, but in the wrong direction.

"Carlsons'!" She shivered and pulled the strings to the hood of her jacket tighter around her ears. That path was narrow, but it was short. She could lead Dakota if she had to. Besides, cutting through their fields would take a good ten miles off the trip.

Dakota covered the ground quickly, pushing easily through the trees on the narrow trail. Kara avoided overhead branches by lying as flat as she could against the horse's neck. When they broke through near the paddock on the Carlsons' land, she reined Dakota in and studied the landscape. The quickest way was through the west pasture, then along the gravel road until they hit the forest service road that would take them over the hill to Pinewood Meadow.

The big horse didn't hesitate, but moved out as if he'd done this all his life. *He probably has,* Kara thought, but, a half hour into the ride, she knew it wouldn't be as easy as she thought. For one thing, it was hard to get her bearings in the stark, white landscape. Once the Carlsons' farmhouse was out of sight, she had trouble finding the narrow strip of country road.

Dakota must have sensed her hesitation; he pulled against the bit, obviously wanting to pick up the pace. Open country to him meant a nice, brisk run, but she couldn't chance it. If they missed the road, they'd wind up lost in the mountains.

"Whoa." She tugged on the reins, and the big gelding reluctantly obeyed.

"I don't know about you," she told her restless companion, "but I'm hungry." And thirsty, she suddenly realized. It had been stupid to leave the house without eating and drinking first. Not to mention the fact that she didn't dare get off her horse. Dakota was too tall for her to remount alone, and there wasn't a stump in sight.

By twisting in the saddle, she was able to untie a canteen. The water tasted a little brackish, but she didn't care. Dakota snorted with impatience as she dug through the saddlebags for a fruit roll and a piece of jerky. *Some breakfast!* But it would have to do.

She nudged the gelding's sides with the heels of her boots, sending him forward, then at an angle to the right. He plowed through the snow up over his hocks like it was no big deal, and she knew she had chosen the right horse. Lily would never have made it.

A few minutes later, they found the road. Kara breathed a sigh of relief and eased up on the reins. Dakota obliged by quickening his pace and took them swiftly along, slowing only a little when the track began to climb into the woods. They crossed a narrow wooden bridge, and she guided the gelding down to the water's edge. He drank gratefully, then turned and stripped a mouthful of needles from the nearest pine tree.

Wakara could have kicked herself again for not bringing more grain.

"Hang on, boy. We'll be at Eagle Lodge before you know it."

18

THE SKY HAD LIGHTENED to a pale shade of gray when Wakara rode into Pinewood Meadow. Her hands were so numb she couldn't feel the reins, and her feet inside her boots felt like blocks of ice. Dakota stopped at the trailhead and would go no farther. His breath sent whiffs of steam into the thin cold air. Every time she tried to urge him on, he danced backward trying to turn away. Her own breath puffed into the wool lining of her parka hood.

"You remember, don't you, boy?" Pinewood Meadow was where they had found the horses grazing after the fire. Both Dakota and Lily had made a dash up the narrow Pine Creek trail through smoke and flames. No wonder he was spooked about going down there again. She patted his neck and turned him away from the trail. She knew she should dismount and get them both something to eat and drink, but one look around the barren landscape told her she'd never get back on again.

She shifted in the saddle and cried out as pain shot up her back and down both legs. Her eyes stung and she could hardly keep them open. What time was it? She knew she'd been riding for hours, but the weak winter light made it hard to tell. Besides, her head felt as if someone had replaced her brain with a wad of cotton.

She forced herself to stretch in the saddle, then turned Dakota toward the water trough at the far corner of the meadow. He nuzzled aside several inches of snow, popped through a thin coating of ice, and drank greedily while she reached for her own canteen. With any other horse she would have had to find some way to warm the water so he didn't get a bellyache, but Dakota had been raised in Alaska. "He's used to the cold," Colin had said, "and he's got an iron gut."

Please, God, let that be true.

She pulled off her gloves with her teeth and stuck her hands under her armpits to warm them. She winced as needles of pain shot through her fingers and wrists. When she could finally use her fingers, she undid one of the saddle-bags, grabbed a small, round container of grain, and spread half the contents on the ground. Dakota scarfed it up before she'd even opened her own snack, and was eagerly searching the ground for more.

Kara chuckled and patted his neck again. "Later, boy, we've still got a ways to go."

She threw another handful of peanuts and raisins into her mouth, then zipped the bag shut and stowed it in her pack. When she had rubbed some feeling back into her legs, she turned Dakota once more toward the trailhead. This time he hesitated but didn't fight as she directed him down the trail.

Kara looked for the spot where they had discovered Colin and Anne hiding in a cave after the fire, but all the trees and brush at the beginning of the trail looked different in the bright white snow.

Snow also helped to mask the devastation from the fire, but she could hardly stand to look at the ruined forest. Stark,

140

black skeletons were all that remained of the trees still standing. As Dad had said, the trail was clear of fallen limbs, but the underbrush on the cliff side was gone, leaving a head-spinning view of the valley below.

Dakota picked his way carefully down the narrow, switch-back trail, while Wakara kept her eyes straight ahead and tried to concentrate on her goal. Dad and Greg—finding them was the only thing that mattered. "Please, God, let them be at the lodge." She felt a surge of hope that quickly died as questions plagued her. If they were there, why didn't they answer her calls? The radio equipment had just been repaired. There was no way it should be malfunctioning again. She knew the problem wasn't with the set in Lariat— she had talked to Tia, and the reception had been fine. That meant either Dad wasn't there to hear her call, or for some reason was unable to answer.

Flutters of anticipation and fear racked her belly as the trail flattened out and they came into the clearing by Otter Lake. Kara gasped. Greg had told her the fire had burned the hottest here, but she wasn't prepared for the devastation she saw around her. Everything green was gone. No live trees, no bushes—nothing to break up the stark landscape except for tangles of snow-covered branches, heaped like piles of pickup sticks scattered over the forest floor.

The lake had shrunk to a dull, dark pool. A blanket of snow covered the barren ground, with only a few blackened tree stumps sticking up like markers in a graveyard. She realized again what a miracle it was that Colin and Anne had gotten out alive.

Dakota plodded, head down, along the familiar route. Every so often he would snort and shake his head as if trying to rid his nostrils of some putrid smell. Kara loosened the hood of her parka and risked a breath of the cold air.

It smelled vaguely of damp soot, and she knew that for a horse the odor would be several times as strong.

As the ground leveled out, Dakota picked up his pace. Then, as they neared Eagle Lodge, he plowed through the snow as if his huge feet were merely parting water. Kara laughed as his head came up and his ears began to twitch like radar. "We're getting close now, aren't we, boy?" But her spirits plummeted again as they broke out of the meadow onto the narrow landing strip that ran between the river and the lodge.

"Whoa." She halted Dakota at the base of the hill. He strained at the bit, sensing food and shelter at the familiar hundred-year-old barn.

"Easy, boy. Just let me check it out." She scanned the property first. The wooden fence on the corral was charred, and the poles had toppled to the ground. The airplane hangar and outside stalls were scorched as well, but at least they were standing. Still, she could tell Dad and Greg hadn't even begun to work on the corral.

She urged the horse forward and he responded instantly, heading quickly uphill toward the barn. Kara had a good view of the lodge from here, and her stomach churned in disappointment. There was no lantern light shining from the windows, and no smoke pouring from the chimney.

"They aren't there." She wanted to lie down and cry. Instead, she reined Dakota in at the entrance to the barn and listened carefully for any sound of intruders. The small, battered door had been patched with strips of plywood after a bear broke it down to go after the grain. The last thing she wanted was to face a bear or cougar holed up in there. If there were any animals lurking in the shadows, she'd rather know it now, while they were still in the open.

The barn lay dark and silent. Nothing stirred in the dim interior, and Dakota tugged at the bit, eager to get inside.

Wakara knew if anything was in there, the horse would sense it first.

She loosened the reins and ducked under the overhang as Dakota made a sharp right turn and headed straight for his usual stall. Kara breathed a sigh of relief when she saw a pile of loose hay in the feeder. The bin in the next stall also held hay, and a bucket of grain stood in the corner by the tack box.

"Well, boy, looks like you'll be well fed, anyway," she said as he lowered his head and nipped up a mouthful of hay.

She lowered her backpack to the floor and bit back a cry of pain as she eased one leg over the saddle horn, turned, and slid to the ground. When her feet touched the ground, she had to grab the saddle and hang on. It took long, agonizing minutes for feeling to return to her legs and feet. She felt the tears sliding warm and wet down her frosted cheeks.

Not now! she lectured herself. *Can't give in. Have to think.* But her mind didn't seem to want to function any better than her feet.

She felt stiff as a Popsicle stick as she unhooked the straps and eased the bit out of Dakota's mouth, leaving the head-stall in place. "Sorry, boy, but you're going to have to stay saddled for now—I don't think I can lift it off you." She dragged her pack out of the stall and sank to the floor.

When she awoke, the cold light filtering through the grimy windows told her it was full day. Dakota had finished his breakfast and snoozed contentedly, head down, eyes closed, with one back foot cocked. Her groan when she tried to move should have wakened the dead, but the horse didn't even flinch.

"Oh, brother, I wish it were that easy!" She gripped the chain across the stall door and pulled herself to her feet. When she was sure she could stand, she tried a few tentative steps, still holding on to anything within reach. After a couple of minutes she was able to stagger down the aisle and out the barn door. "Now I know how a cowboy feels after a six-day cattle drive."

She winced as she stepped into the midday sun. Light reflecting off the pristine snow caused a moment of blindness. She blinked several times, then brought one hand to her forehead and squinted up at the lodge. It seemed to stare back at her with empty, vacant eyes. Kara took a deep breath and pushed forward. Picking a spot where she thought the path should be, she plodded slowly up the hill.

They hadn't bothered to lock the door, but except for two plates and two ceramic mugs stacked in the sink, they had left the place clean. Kara nearly yelped with joy when she saw several hunks of charred wood still in the big fireplace, and a stack of kindling along with a package of fire starters in the wood box.

She quickly made a fire, stripped off her jacket and boots, and huddled as close as she could without frying her skin. When she finally felt warm again, she hung a pot of water from the iron pole, then pushed it over the flames. Hot chocolate would taste better than coffee right now. She drank a full cup, and then added hot water to a package of freeze-dried chicken noodle soup. It tasted as good as a prime rib dinner.

Her hunger finally satisfied, she explored the rest of the lodge. The other rooms smelled faintly of smoke, but none of them had been used since the guys had brought out all of the stuff she and Ryan had packed up before the fire. Dad and Greg had probably spread their sleeping bags in front of the fireplace to conserve fuel. She found some of their clothes and gear stored in the hall closet, then searched the kitchen and discovered a good supply of dried and canned food.

She saved the radio room until last. As she suspected, the equipment looked fine, but the only way to really find out was to try to use it.

Should she try to call home? She frowned at the thought. She still hadn't found Dad and Greg, so there was nothing to report. Besides, by now Colin and Anne knew she was gone and were probably not in a very good mood. *Why stir up a hornet's nest?*

She felt a pinprick of guilt, but she brushed it aside. She had left a note, so they couldn't be nearly as worried about her as she was about Dad and Greg. The men weren't here, their horses weren't in the barn, and no one had heard from them since the first storm.

Fear struck deep and as hard as a fist in her gut. *Stay calm. Panic never solved any problems.* She needed to think, but she was so tired!

She pressed her head against the picture window in the dining room and closed her eyes. "God, please," she prayed out loud, "if all wisdom comes from You, then please, please, help me!"

Be still and wait.

The gentle whisper was not what she wanted to hear. She opened her eyes and stared across the deck, out over the hillside, past the shored-up barn to the river, where it disappeared around a bend into the trees. A smooth blanket of snow covered the earth as far as her eyes could see. She knew a closer look would reveal the tracks of small animals and birds, but hers and Dakota's were the only larger tracks to be seen.

She lifted her gaze to the jagged Blue Mountains. Deep in the next valley lay Cutter's Gap, a thickly wooded area of fir, blue spruce, and ponderosa pine. If she remembered right from the map the guys had studied before they left, it was in that area they had planned to scout for elk. How much had the fire changed it? She couldn't even guess. But Dad and Greg were out there. They'd been out there for nearly three days in blizzard conditions, and the queasy feeling in her stomach still told her there was something terribly wrong.

She had just pushed away from the window, when she heard Dakota whinny.

"Dad!" She flew to the door and ran out onto the porch in time to see a lone rider come into view around the bend.

The cold bit deeply into her flannel-covered arms and bootless feet. She spun around and hurried back inside. She thrust her feet back into her boots, shoved her arms into her parka, and dashed outside again.

The rider sat slumped over in the saddle, and the horse was one she didn't recognize from this distance. She hesitated only a moment. Maybe someone had found them and was coming here for help. She jumped off the deck, legs churning wildly, and plunged down the hill. With any luck she would beat the rider to the barn.

19

"COLIN!"

Her surprised yelp caused his horse to shy, and she grabbed the bridle to steady the animal. "What are you doing here? How did you get here so fast?"

The look on his face caused her to release the horse and back away.

He swung down from the saddle, and she winced at the shock of pain that creased his forehead. "I know how you feel." She grabbed the bridle again so Colin could get his balance. "It's a long ride."

The look he gave her would have melted ice. "No, Wakara, you don't know how I feel!" He shook his head, leaned his face against the horse's neck, then turned and grabbed her by the shoulders. "Of all the idiotic ideas! How could you pull such a stunt?" He gave her a hard shake, then abruptly dropped his hands.

Kara felt stunned. Her mouth went dry, and all she could do was stare at him. She had expected him to be upset, but she'd never seen him this angry before.

"What exactly did you expect to accomplish by coming up here alone?" His voice was low and rough, his hands clenched into fists at his sides. She had never seen him so angry. "Or did you want to scare Anne into a heart attack, and, just for kicks, drag me out into the middle of nowhere during the worst weather of the century?" He yanked off his hat and swiped one wrist across his forehead.

He's sweating. Wakara stared in amazement, then some of what he said sunk in, and she finally found her voice. "Anne?"

She hadn't meant it to come out in such a pitiful squeak, but Colin's eyes softened. "She's okay. We found your note."

Then what's the big deal? She frowned. "Greg and Dad aren't here, Colin, which means they're somewhere out there," she gestured toward the northeast, "which also means they're either lost or trapped."

Colin's eyes narrowed again and he slapped his hat against his thigh. "And what are you—a one-woman Search-and-Rescue team?"

Wakara felt the heat flood from her neck to her face. "I didn't think . . ."

Again he cut her off. "Oh, now there's a revelation—you didn't think!" His eyes flashed fire. "Well, I thought about it. All the way here I thought about finding you alongside the trail frozen to death—or worse, not finding you at all." He turned away and yanked the saddlebags off his horse.

Her heart was drumming so hard she thought her chest would explode. "Colin Jones, I am not a child! I can take care of myself."

He snorted. "Right."

Furious, she wanted to smack him. Instead, she grabbed his arm, and he swung around to face her, but this time she got her licks in first. "Anyway, who died and made you my keeper?" She hated the nasty tone that had crept into her voice, but she couldn't seem to stop it. "You are not my father or my brother. You're only here because Dad hired you to work the stock. If you cared a thing about my family, you'd be helping me find them instead of standing here lecturing me like I was four years old."

He stiffened, and his eyes went cold, but instead of yelling back at her, he shouldered his pack and took hold of the horse's bridle. When he finally spoke, his voice was quiet and controlled. "Look, can we talk about this later? I've got to get this horse fed and watered, and I could use some food myself."

Fine. If he didn't want to settle it, that was okay by her. She turned and followed him into the barn. Dakota nickered a welcome and went back to munching hay.

Wakara watched Colin unsaddle the Appaloosa, then hang the bridle and saddlebags from a hook on the wall. Automatically, she handed him a brush from the tack box, then filled a water bucket and grabbed an armload of hay. Neither of them spoke while Colin picked packed snow out of the horse's feet, then went into Dakota's stall.

When he saw Dakota still saddled, he frowned. "How long have you been here?"

Kara ignored his tone. "Long enough. I was just too tired."

Colin sighed and reached for the cinch to unbuckle the saddle, but Kara laid a hand on his arm. "I'll do it." She kept her voice soft. When he looked at her, she nodded toward the lodge. "There's a fire and hot water for coffee. I've already rested."

He hesitated, then nodded, and she could tell he was about to fall asleep on his feet. "Okay, I won't argue with you."

Before she could turn away, he reached out and touched her cheek. "For what it's worth, Anne called the sheriff again. He's getting a posse together, but there's another storm headed in, and they aren't sure how quickly they'll get here."

She felt tears sting her eyes. "We can't wait, Colin. What if they're injured? I can't just sit back and wait for Sheriff Lassen to get his rear in gear."

To her surprise, Colin burst out laughing. "Wakara, you're amazing." He shook his head. "Tell you what, when I get some strength back, I'll take Dakota and see what I can find. You keep the fire going and the coffee hot, and send in the cavalry when they get here. Deal?"

Kara could only stare as he turned away and moved slowly out of the barn.

Keep the fire going? Stay at the lodge? He couldn't be serious! She gritted her teeth, followed him to the doorway, and watched him stagger up the hill, glad he couldn't see her face.

She waited until she heard the screen door slam, the noise bouncing like buckshot off the mountain. "In your dreams, Colin Jones!" she snarled, and hurried back to Dakota's stall. As she tightened the cinch on the saddle, she pictured Colin taking off his jacket and boots, then warming himself in front of the fire. She tied the saddlebags across the horse's rump. *Now he's in the kitchen scrounging up food.* She warmed the bit by rubbing it with the tail of her flannel shirt, then slipped it into the gelding's mouth and fastened it to the headstall. *He's pouring water into instant coffee. Stirring soup into another mug.*

She kicked off her boots, grabbed an extra pair of socks from her backpack, and changed quickly. *Eating, drinking, rubbing his eyes.* "Go to sleep, Colin," she whispered. She yanked on dry gloves, shouldered her pack, and led the reluctant gelding to the barn door.

The other horse, his muzzle buried in a pile of hay, ignored them. So far, so good.

She peeked around the corner, gazing intently toward the lodge. She hadn't bothered with a lantern, and it appeared Colin hadn't either, because no light came from behind the wide, plate glass window. She strained to see inside, but the view from here was limited. She would just have to take a chance that he was preoccupied with feeding his face, or better yet, fast asleep and snoring. She giggled at the image of Colin lounging on the sofa, hat pulled low over his eyes, his breath rattling the rafters. When her chuckles unexpectedly turned to tears, she dashed them away with the back of her hand and led Dakota around the corner to the far side of the barn. When she was sure they were out of sight of the lodge, she stepped up on a tree stump and into the saddle.

She guided Dakota east, then north, across the wooden bridge. When he hesitated, turning automatically onto the river trail, she pulled his head around and urged him forward into the wind.

It seemed they'd been riding for hours when she recognized the rock formations that told her they were entering Cutter's Gap. The ridge above them looked bare, pocked by carcasses of blackened trees, with no sign of the sturdy mountain goats that usually grazed there. But the valley they entered was still green, with stands of fir and snow-covered pine, interspersed with wild rhododendrons and azaleas. Kara could see where the fire had jumped the ridge and continued on its raging path toward Otter Lake, missing this valley completely.

As they rode on, the sky grew dark. Once she thought she heard someone scream. She brought Dakota to a halt, but there was only silence. Angry, low clouds rolled in from the west, and lace-shaped snowflakes sprinkled the horse's mane. Any other time Wakara would have gasped in awe at the beauty and power of nature. Now all she felt was a swift kick of fear.

Dakota's head stayed down, his breathing rapid. She reached around to rub his chest and found it foamy with sweat. She felt an instant regret. "I'm sorry, boy. We'll find a place to stop."

Another look at the sky told her they needed to find shelter—fast!

She urged the tired horse into a stand of trees. A cave would be better, she thought. There was always the danger of a tree limb crashing down on them—a widow-maker. Loggers had made up that term for branches that snapped off in the cold and crushed anyone standing in the way. She shuddered and studied the area around them in the fading light. *Well, Wako, now it's time to see if you learned anything from your own survival course.*

The most important thing was warmth, and she headed off on foot to gather as much wood as possible. She found a broken tree branch, then another, and soon had enough to make the frame for a small shelter. She worked quickly, piling on pine boughs and lining the floor with a thick layer of cedar. She pulled off Dakota's saddle, spread the saddle pad on top of the branches, and then added another layer of cedar.

With another broken branch she dug out a small circle at the entrance to her shelter, then piled rocks for a windbreak and started a fire. She wanted nothing more than to huddle in its warmth, eat some of her meager provisions, and fall asleep, but one glance toward the clearing told her she didn't dare.

It had come on so fast. Like someone had turned over one of those paperweights, and poof, instant snowstorm.

Using the saddle cinch to secure Dakota's two blankets to his back, she fed him the last of the grain, then poured water from one of the canteens into the empty container. He sucked greedily, and she gently rubbed his neck. "Sorry, boy, I didn't mean to get you into this." She tried to quiet her conscience with the thought that he'd already eaten at least two pads of hay today. That, plus the grain and blankets, would help to keep him warm. "You'll probably be more comfortable than I will."

As if to verify the fact, Dakota snorted, cocked one back foot, and closed his eyes.

Darkness fell as quickly as the snow, and Kara thought the temperature had dropped at least 20 degrees. She shivered as the cold seeped into her bones, and the fire drew her like a moth to a flame.

A layer of snow packed over the pine boughs would help insulate the shelter, but she didn't have the strength. She quickly stowed her saddlebags and pack in the back of the shelter and crawled in after them. It didn't leave much room to sit, let alone lie down, but the crowded conditions would keep her warmer, and the packs would stay dry.

She tugged off her boots. Thank God she had brought along her fur-lined slippers. They would help thaw out her feet. She pulled them on, along with a clean pair of thick, wool socks. The chicken soup she'd had for lunch was a distant memory. She finished off one package of trail mix and closed her eyes. A hamburger or a huge bowl of Anne's chili would sure taste good right now.

Thinking back on her hasty exit, she realized that Colin might very well have come after her, and she felt another pang of guilt. All she wanted to do was find Dad and Greg. Had she caused more trouble instead?

She groaned and lay against the backpack, bending her knees and shifting her feet to the side so they wouldn't land in the fire. "I'm so tired! Take care of them, God, please? And Colin too."

Maybe he saw the storm coming and stayed at Eagle Lodge. But she had a gut feeling he had followed her.

No one is responsible for this mess but you. The words she had spoken to Ryan haunted her dreams.

20

A SOUND LIKE A WOMAN'S SCREAM shattered the night. Wakara bolted upright, hit her head on a pole, and nearly overturned the shelter. Lightning bolts of fear shot through her as the scream came again, closer this time; a long, drawn out *Heeellp* rising in pitch, then swallowed by the still, cold air. The fire had burned down to embers. It had stopped snowing, and she could just make out Dakota's form as he whinnied and stamped around the tree, trying to break free of his ties.

Her heart was galloping like a million hoofbeats in her chest. Then she smelled it—the damp, unwashed smell of a wild animal. Only one thing in the woods sounded and smelled like that.

Cougar!

Dakota became even more agitated as moonlight filtered through the trees, bouncing shadows off the snow. Kara felt like she was frozen to the ground. Her mouth was as dry as a dusty rag, and it hurt to breathe. One of the shadows moved outside, jolting her to action.

"EEAYAH!" she yelled at the top of her lungs. She scrambled around, grabbed a piece of firewood, and threw it. "Go on!" she screamed and threw another. "Get out of here!"

The shadow growled and backed away, but didn't leave. Quickly, she added a handful of twigs and moss to the embers in her fire pit and blew gently on the flames. *Don't panic. Don't panic.* She kept repeating it over and over. There was no doubt in her mind that the cat would go after Dakota first, then, maybe, have her for dessert.

When she had the fire built up enough to offer some protection, she groped for the stick she'd used to dig the pit. One chance, that's all she'd have. Her hands were shaking, and she was so cold she didn't even know if her legs would support her. *Please, God. I can't do this on my own.* Hot tears ran down her cheeks, but she didn't even try to wipe them away. She sniffed and rolled to her knees. Her muscles cramped, and she let out a scream of pain. The shadow darted through the trees in front of her and became the biggest cougar she'd ever seen.

Dakota went ballistic. Kicking and jerking at the rope, he finally broke free, nearly trampling the shelter as he ran. Wakara knew she had to act—NOW—before the cougar went after him.

She quickly stuck the pointed end of the stick in the fire, then scrambled out of the shelter, waving her arms and yelling at the top of her lungs. It felt like slow motion as she grabbed the flaming stick, drew back her arm, and fired it like a javelin at the crouching animal.

Later, she would have to admit she wasn't sure what happened next. The big cat yowled once, then was gone, leaving behind huge footprints and the smell of scorched fur.

She wasn't sure how long she huddled in the shelter, trying to get warm. She cried and prayed. When her muscles finally stopped quivering, the sky was turning light. Movement in the bushes sent her heart skipping again, but a soft snort told her Dakota was back.

"Thank you, God!"

She crawled out of the shelter and wrapped her arms around the big gelding's neck, breathing in the sweet, damp smell. "Good boy. You're a good horse; I knew you wouldn't leave me."

She forced herself to make coffee, ate a candy bar and another fruit roll, then stuck a wad of jerky in her jacket pocket to chew on as she rode. Dakota was quietly munching grass from the half-circle he'd trampled around his tree. It wasn't much, but she let him eat, then offered him the last of the water in one canteen.

"Hang on, boy," she told him as she led him into the clearing. She climbed a large rock and stepped into the saddle. "If we don't find them by noon, we'll turn back."

An hour later, she saw the smoke.

She spotted it from the top of a hill. At first it looked like mist rising from the valley floor, but as she watched, it curled and darkened. Then the wind changed and she picked up the distinctive campfire smell.

Relief flooded through her, making her legs tremble as she stood in the stirrups. "DAD!" she shouted and spurred Dakota forward, pulling him up just in time to keep from plunging down a steep ravine. Her heart thudded against her ribs as she studied the trampled ground, where a huge gash in the earth showed that something or someone had gone over the side.

She filled her lungs with air and screamed as loud as she could. "DAD!"

"Wakara? Here!"

When he stepped into her line of vision, she gasped. It looked as if he came right out of the side of the mountain.

157

He shielded his eyes, looking up at her and motioning her away. "Get back. Don't go near the edge—it isn't stable."

"How do I get down there?"

He motioned her around, through another stand of trees. "It flattens out on the other side. Follow the tree line to the left. You'll find the way."

Ten minutes later, she slid off Dakota into her father's arms.

After a long hug, he eased her away. "Boy, Sugar Bear, am I glad to see you."

She grinned. "I'm glad to see you too. Even if you do look like a run-over porcupine."

He grimaced and ran one hand over his face. It was red from the cold and covered with thick, black stubble. "Haven't shaved in awhile."

He looked over her shoulder, shielding his eyes to study the area above the ravine. "Where are the others?"

There was nothing to do but tell him the truth. And if she lived to be a hundred, she never again wanted to see that look in his eyes.

His reddened skin turned pale as he backed away and slumped against a boulder. "I don't believe this. Wakara Sheridan, whatever possessed you to pull such a stunt?"

A loud groan made the skin on the back of Kara's neck tingle and broke off any further attempt at explanation.

"Where's Greg?"

"In there." Dad nodded toward the entrance to a small cave nestled back in among the rocks. "His horse went over the edge. Greg must have hit his head. When I got to him, he was unconscious, and the horse was gone."

He hurried into the cave. Wakara followed, stepping around the windbreak Dad had built out of snow blocks.

Greg lay on a bed of cedar boughs, wrapped in the saddle blanket Anne had given him for his birthday.

Kara knelt beside him. "Greg?" He moaned again but didn't open his eyes.

"He's been like that for three days. All I could do was keep him warm, get some water down him, and pray. There was no way I could leave him to get help, even when the weather cooperated. That's why I was hoping . . ."

She winced. "I know. You were hoping I had brought the Search-and-Rescue team." She hated the look of desperation on his face. His eyes were red-rimmed, his mouth white, and his shoulders slumped with exhaustion.

He nodded, then sat down close to Greg. With his back to the wall of the cave, he closed his eyes.

Kara studied the interior of the cave. It made a great shelter, and with the fire protected on all four sides by rock and snow, it was actually warm. She rummaged through their provisions, found an instant coffee bag, and poured water from the pot by the fire into two tin cups.

"Thanks, Sugar Bear. Sorry I can't offer you a hamburger. I'm afraid provisions are running pretty low."

She answered his weak grin with one of her own. "The coffee tastes good. But then, so would a boiled sock." She sighed and sat down on the other side of Greg, leaning back against the wall. Her muscles kept cramping, and her feet inside her boots were damp and cold.

She felt herself dozing and sat up straight. What was she doing? They had to get Greg out of there before it started snowing again. "I've got Dakota, Dad. He can easily carry Greg. You and I can ride double."

Dad just looked at her, that look of resignation burning in his eyes. "We can't move him, Wakara. He has a head injury. He'd never survive the ride."

"You're right. They'll have to bring in the chopper."

Dad shook his head. "They won't. For the same reason I couldn't fire the rifle to attract attention."

"Avalanche."

He nodded. "Our only hope is for them to come in with a toboggan, stabilize his head and neck . . ."

Kara was thinking fast. "And get him back to Eagle Lodge. A chopper could land there easily, and with no danger of starting a slide." Joy surged through her as she scrambled to her feet. "I'm out of here!"

"In your dreams."

Kara blinked. She had never heard Dad say that before. "What?"

"If you think you are going anywhere, young lady, you are sadly mistaken." He was sitting up now, looking angrier than she'd ever seen him. "I have one of my children lying here unconscious—I will not risk your life by allowing you to go back out there alone. We stay here, Wakara, and we wait for help."

Close your mouth, Wakara, you'll catch a fly. She could hear Mom's voice as if she were standing in the back of the cave. She closed her mouth, then opened it again. "But Dad, I'm not really alone."

He held up one hand to silence her. "God got you this far, Wakara, but He expects you to use some common sense. If you had thought a little more about your actions in the last day or so, you would have stayed with your little brother and let the sheriff do his job."

She felt like he had slapped her. "I called him, Dad. He wouldn't do his job!" Her voice squeaked on a sob. "He told me to relax, that you were fine! He was too busy to come out here, then the weather got bad again. Somebody had to do something!"

Dad just sighed and shook his head. "Come here." He held out his arms, and she let him pull her against his chest. She wanted to sob for an hour, then crawl into bed and sleep for a week.

But Dad wasn't through. "I know you meant well, but unfortunately your coming here hasn't accomplished anything except to have one more person missing. Not to mention that Anne and Colin must be going out of their minds with worry."

"Colin!" She pushed back and dried her tears on the sleeve of her jacket. "That's what I meant when I said I wasn't alone. He's probably right behind me." *If he didn't get lost in last night's blizzard.* She didn't voice that thought. "He told me Anne called the sheriff before he left. They should be on their way, Dad. They should be at the lodge by now!"

Now it was Dad's turn to stare at her with his mouth open. She stifled a giggle. Now was not the time to laugh, either.

"Colin is at the lodge?"

"Uh, I doubt it. He probably followed me as soon as the weather cleared." Except he had been pretty upset. What if he had decided to just let her be the idiot he thought she was and go home? No, he wouldn't do that with Dad and Greg still missing.

"Can he follow your tracks?"

"Yes. At least the ones I made today." She rushed on before he could say anything more. "I can follow them too. I can meet him and send him back for the others."

Dad was already shaking his head, so she hurried on, "It's only a few miles. I'd have been here yesterday if it weren't for the storm. We can get Greg out of here, Dad. We can get him out today!"

Dad's mouth was set in that stubborn line that meant he'd made up his mind and was not about to budge.

Kara sighed. "I know it wasn't very responsible to take off on my own like that. But, no matter what the others said, I knew something was wrong. And look at Greg!"

He laid a hand against her cheek. "And what would have happened if you had waited one more day?"

161

Her shoulders slumped. "I guess the sheriff would have sent out Search-and-Rescue as soon as the weather cleared. But how long do you think it would have taken them to find you? That other blizzard hit, and you said yourself you couldn't fire the rifle."

Greg groaned again. Dad knelt down beside him and lay two fingers against the side of his neck. "He's getting weaker." A tear dripped onto the sleeve of his jacket.

Kara went outside, added wood to the fire, and got a drink from her own canteen. When she came back in, she handed Dad a hunk of jerky. "The sky is clear. You can see forever. Let me go, please. If I don't find help by this afternoon, I'll turn back, I promise."

"Three hours." She could hear the pain in his voice. "One cloud in the sky, and you're back here."

"Got it." She hugged him hard and hobbled out of the cave. Now if only her muscles would cooperate and let her get back on the horse.

21

DAKOTA WAS AS EXHAUSTED as she was. In spite of the urgency of their mission, Kara let him pick his own pace. "This is the last trip, boy, I promise." She hoped it was the truth.

Twenty minutes later the horse's ears picked up, and so did his step. Kara felt a thrill of excitement as the lone rider came around the bend. She spurred the gelding on through the churned-up snow, and the two horses nearly collided. In a blur of motion, Colin jumped down and pulled her out of the saddle. She cringed, expecting him to yell at her. Instead he drew her into a tight hug and refused to let her go. With her ear pressed to his chest, she could hear his heartbeat racing along with her own.

Tears of relief flooded her eyes, and she didn't even try to wipe them away. She lifted her head. "Colin, I'm *so* sorry. I'm glad you're okay."

"Shh." He hushed her, pulled her even closer for a moment, then abruptly let her go. "Wakara." His voice was raspy. He pushed away and stepped back, hands dangling by his side. "Don't ever do that again."

She had expected him to be angry. Instead, he looked scared and hurt and relieved all at the same time. It reminded her of the stray pup Greg had once brought home; it had that same sad-eyed, wistful stare.

Dad and Greg! "I found them, Colin. Greg's hurt really bad."

She explained the situation while Colin cupped his hands and gave her a leg up into the saddle, then mounted his own horse.

"I called Search-and-Rescue. They should be at the lodge by now. Just tell them to follow our tracks in." He spun the horse around to face her. "Go back to Eagle Lodge and stay there, Wakara, please. Dakota needs rest, and someone needs to call Anne."

This time she didn't argue. "I'll build up the fire. Everyone will need coffee and food."

His smile warmed her all over. "Thanks, Wakara. Your dad and Greg will be out of there in no time."

"Please God, let that be true," she whispered as she spurred the reluctant Dakota toward Eagle Lodge.

The sheriff and his men were just coming down the hill. Wakara gave them directions, then led Dakota to his stall. After filling the water bucket and giving him a double portion of fresh hay, she hurried up the hill.

The next four hours were the longest of her life.

Twice she started to saddle Dakota and go after the men. Both times she got down on her knees and prayed instead. Finally, she fell asleep, and the next thing she heard was the clatter of helicopter blades as the huge machine settled easily on the landing strip down by the river.

She set the coffeepot aside and stirred powdered soup into the kettle of hot water, grabbed her coat, and rushed outside in time to see two men on skis guiding a travois with Greg strapped inside. Dad and Colin rode slowly behind.

Dad went with Greg in the chopper. Colin slipped one arm around her shoulder. "Greg woke up for a few minutes and knew who we were. That's a good sign."

164

Colin helped her pass around mugs of hot coffee and soup to Sheriff Lassen and his men, then went into the radio room. When he came out, he told her, "Bud Davis is bringing a trailer up to Pinewood Meadow."

Kara sighed. "Whew. That's a relief. I've had enough of that saddle to last a lifetime."

Colin laughed. "Sure. I'll give you forty-eight hours and you'll be on Lily's back. Bet?"

She grinned and stuck her tongue out at him. "No bets, Mister Smarty, you're probably right." She yawned. "But right now I think I could sleep for a week."

When they got home, she finished off two helpings of vegetable beef stew, crawled into bed, and slept for twenty-four hours. Even then, when the phone on her bed table jangled her awake, she wanted to throw it across the room. "Hello?"

"Wakara? You sound like a sick frog. What's up? Pops said your brother's in the hospital, and he wouldn't let me call until now."

Kara grinned. "Sorry, Tia. I'm still kind of out of it. Can I call you back?"

"I guess."

Her friend sounded so disappointed, Kara rushed on, "Ten minutes, I promise."

Tia's voice brightened. "Okay. Talk to you in ten."

The click in her ear told her Tia had hung up. Wakara plopped back down on the pillow. She still felt sleepy and a little disoriented. Then it hit her. *Greg!*

She jumped up, pulled on a pair of sweats, and dashed downstairs. "Dad? Anne? Where is everyone?"

"In here."

She hurried into the kitchen. Anne was standing at the stove, and for the first time Kara noticed the enticing aroma of bacon and eggs.

"Food!"

Anne nodded. "You will be hungry now. I have made enough for two."

"Thanks." Kara wasn't sure what else to say. She knew she had worried Anne by leaving in the night. After that, the fire, and the episode with Ryan, she was surprised the woman was still around.

She took a plate from the cupboard and held it out for the cook to fill. "Anne? I just want to say I'm sorry for scaring you. I shouldn't have left that way."

"You are forgiven." Anne smiled and heaped scrambled eggs onto Wakara's plate. "Now eat. You must stay strong."

Kara carried her plate to the table, filled a mug with coffee, and sat down. She was hungrier than she'd ever been in her life, but there was so much she needed to know. "I can't believe I slept that long! Where is everybody? Have you heard a report on Greg?"

Anne sat a plate of toast next to Kara's coffee cup and pulled out a chair. "Greg is awake, but he is still very sick. Your father is with him. Colin cares for the stock, and Ryan stays with Timmy's family."

The back door squeaked open, and Colin stepped in, followed by a rush of cold air. "Hey, Sleeping Beauty, you're awake."

Kara grinned. "The prince has been here and gone." She chewed another bite of egg, then set down her fork. "How's Dakota? He's not lame or anything, is he?"

"Dakota's just fine, Miss Kara, ma'am. So am I, now that you ask."

Kara rolled her eyes. "That's only obvious. Want some breakfast? Anne made enough for six men."

She spread jam on a second piece of toast and handed it to him. He wolfed it down in three bites.

"I've eaten, but thanks." He grinned and wiped crumbs from his mouth. "I have to wash up. If you want a ride to the hospital, the bus leaves in twenty minutes."

She gulped down her coffee and ran upstairs to shower and wash her hair. She had just pulled on a sweater and a clean pair of jeans when it hit her.

"Oh, my gosh, I forgot to call Tia."

The first time, she got a busy signal. Five minutes later, the phone rang and rang as if no one was home. She hung up just as Colin's pickup rattled over the gravel and into the drive.

Great, she thought, *now Tia will be mad at me.* It seemed like all she'd done lately was upset everyone, even when she tried to do the right thing. Why did life have to be so complicated?

She raced out the door and jumped into the passenger seat. Colin turned on the radio. The truck seemed to bounce in rhythm with a country song, and Wakara cringed as Colin sang along in a voice that would make a dog howl. When he motioned her to join in on a duet, she shook her head and turned the radio off.

"You didn't come after me that night, did you?" The words slipped out without warning, but he didn't seem at all surprised. She watched the pain rush across his face, then settle into an awkward smile.

"No," he said quietly, then paused and turned to look at her. "I started to, you know. But the storm was on us before I could get the Appaloosa saddled."

"Are you still mad?"

He sighed and shook his head. "No, Wakara, I'm not mad. I was then. You scared the spit out of me!" He slapped the steering wheel. "I can't even tell you the thoughts that were going through my head. Then I remembered what I learned at camp, you know, the bumper sticker on my truck?"

She nodded. "Let go and get a grip on God."

"That's right. It works, Wakara. The hardest thing I've ever had to do was let you go that night, but I knew God could take care of you better than I could. It was the only thing that gave me any peace."

He turned the corner onto Main Street, and Kara saw the sign for Mercy Hospital up ahead.

"I prayed for you all night."

She sniffed. "Thanks, I needed it." She thought about the cougar and shuddered.

"I know," he said. "I saw the tracks." His face hardened. "I thought you were dead." He pulled into the parking lot and cut the engine, but kept both hands on the wheel. "When I came around the corner and saw you on Dakota, I almost fell off my horse."

He opened the door, stepped out of the truck, and turned to face her. "I couldn't stand to lose you, Wakara."

She felt glued to her seat. What could she say? *I thought you were dead too, or lost in the storm. I couldn't stand that, Colin. I couldn't stand to lose you either.*

He came around the truck, opened the passenger door, and helped her down. He didn't take her hand, but walked beside her across the parking lot and through the wide automatic doors.

Tia met them in the lobby. "Pops had some errands," she said, "so I came along for the ride." She handed Kara a bouquet of daisies. "I bought these in the gift shop. You can give them to Greg if you want. He's in room 402."

"Thanks, Tia." Wakara pulled her into a hug. "I hadn't even thought about flowers, but you give them to him. He'll like that." She stepped back and studied her friend's beaming face. "I'm sorry I didn't call you back."

Tia linked arms with her and led her to the elevator. "No prob. I just want to know why you get to have all the adventures, and all I get is a term paper?"

Kara stopped in her tracks. "Your paper! Did you finish it?"

Tia grinned. "Oh, yeah." She held up her book bag. "And wait until you read it. This is 4.0 material for sure."

The elevator doors opened and they rushed inside. Kara heard Colin chuckle as he stepped in behind them.

"Floor, ladies?"

"Fourth floor, sir." Tia flashed him a huge smile and hung on to Kara's arm.

22

WAKARA WAS NOT SURPRISED when Tia's history teacher not only gave her an A on her paper, but also encouraged her to enter it in a contest at the University of Oregon.

"First prize is a $2,500 scholarship," Tia crowed. "Do you think I've even got a chance?"

"A chance?" Kara squealed. "I'd say you've got it locked!" She shifted the telephone to the other ear and picked up an extra copy of the manuscript Tia had printed out just for her. "This is good, Tia. You covered all the bases, and the writing is terrific. I bet you're going to get an A in English Comp, too."

When her friend's mom had to make a call, Kara hung up the phone and scanned the pages for the tenth time. It was all there, the history of the Yahi-Yana people, including all Tia had been able to dig up on Ishi and the Lost Ones.

Wakara. Little Moon.

The name was right there on page eight, but it didn't prove a thing about her heritage. In fact, the dates and places where those tribes lived and died only showed that either she wasn't related to the Yahi-Yana people at all, or

170

for some reason Great-grandfather Sheridan had lied about where he found the Indian woman and the baby who would later become his wife.

"Dinner," Dad called from downstairs. She sighed and put the manuscript in her desk drawer.

She was relieved to see Greg sitting next to Colin at the table. He'd come home a few days ago, but the head injury had impaired his hearing and speech and left him as wobbly as a newborn foal.

"We had a good report today," Dad said after he had asked the blessing. "The neurologist says Greg should totally recover." He put one hand over Greg's and squeezed. "It will just take time."

Greg smiled and carefully nodded his head. She had expected him to be frustrated because he couldn't do more, but so far his attitude had been great.

"There is other news." Anne pushed back from the table, limped over to the counter, and returned with a small, hand-addressed envelope.

"Anne, sit still. I could have gotten that for you." Wakara was amazed at how well the Indian woman was getting around without her cast.

Anne handed the letter to Dad and plopped into her chair. "Ugh. With this leg, I have gained twenty pounds. Exercise is good, I think."

Dad nodded. "Just don't overdo. We can't get along without you, Anne. You know that."

He ripped open the envelope and quickly scanned the one-page note. "Well, I'll be switched." He looked up into their expectant faces. "It's from my father, your Grandpa Sheridan."

"From Ireland? Way cool—let me see!" Ryan jumped up and ran around the table, trying to snatch the sheet of paper out of his father's hand.

Kara tugged on his shirt. "Sit down, Ry; let Dad read it."

Dad shook his head. "It's not very long. He just says he's coming to the States and will see us soon." His brow creased in a frown. "No other explanation. I hope he's not ill; if I remember right, he turned seventy-five in June."

"Yippee!" Ryan danced around the kitchen singing, "Grandpa is coming, Grandpa is coming! We're gonna get some neat presents from Ireland!"

"Ryan!" Wakara scolded, but she had to laugh along with everyone else. Grandpa Sheridan had moved to Ireland shortly after she was born, and he had only visited them twice—once when Ryan came along, and again right after Mom had died. That was only a year ago. Like Dad, Kara had to wonder why he was visiting again so soon.

But Ryan was right. Having Grandpa around would be cool. And maybe he could answer some questions about his mother, Wakara's namesake. She felt a surge of excitement as she finished her meal and asked to be excused.

She couldn't wait to call Tia.

Linda Shands is a prolific writer of magazine articles and the author of four adult novels and one nonfiction book. She loves the Oregon wilderness and lives in the small town of Cottage Grove with her husband, a cat, two horses, and twin golden retrievers.

Other titles in the

Wakara of Eagle Lodge series . . .

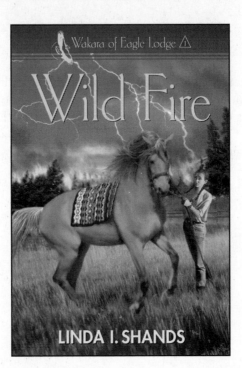

Wild Fire

After her mom's death, Wakara Sheridan tries to
enjoy summer with her horse, her best friend, and the
cute new ranch hand. But just when her family is pulling
together, disaster strikes, and Wakara must survive the
Wild Fire.

0-8007-5746-7

Coming Fall 2001. . .

White Water

Wakara, Tia, Ryan, and Colin fall overboard during a rafting trip. Ryan is swept downstream and Wakara insists on going after him, in spite of all the dangers. When a black bear attacks, will Wakara lose another person she loves?

0-8007-5772-6